THE ECHOES OF FALLEN STARS

IMMORTAL CROWNS

J.D. NETTO

THE ECHOES OF FALLEN STARS

IMMORTAL CROWNS

J.D. NETTO

Dedicated to those who never fit the standard
mold of the world. The crown will
always be yours.

And to Karin Lino Rodrigues,
who never bent her knee to the system.

"In fact, it's not the gods people truly remember.
It's the fear they instill in them."

Lucifer

AUTUMN

THE YEAR 1328
OF THE AGE OF MORTALS

BELLWOUND

CHAPTER ONE

The sun hadn't yet peaked in the sky when Da knocked on my bedroom door. Three knocks. No words. Little did he know, I had been awake for a while already, tossing around in bed. Not that I wanted to go back to sleep. No, my mind wandered in stories of the past.

What are stories if not breath in our lungs? The tales passed down to us shape our future. The ones hidden from us become secrets meant to keep us from harm. Stories and secrets give us purpose, courage, life. Inhaling history, exhaling direction.

Today, the fiftieth day of autumn, was my eighteenth birthday—or as history called it, my Blood-date. A story was the reason I had to get up before the crack of dawn to celebrate my birth, keeping up a tradition written by those I had never met.

A fire still burned in the fireplace, the shy flame strong enough to cast a dancing shadow on the hearth. But it was bound to go out soon, leaving behind only ash and dust. I wondered about the stories that once burned in the hearts of so many but were now forgotten or erased by those who opposed them. How many were out there? Maybe one of those forgotten tales would've gotten me out of waking up so early.

I got up and picked out a black linen shirt and pants from a pile of clothes on the floor. I grabbed a bear-pelt shoulder cape from my wardrobe and met Da downstairs. He waited by the door, next to my muddy boots. Ma would've chopped my head off if I had walked in the house with them yesterday.

Da wore black from head to toe, his hair braided down his back—a pattern I knew but had never seen him wear. His hair was woven like the roots of a bitterlie tree, random thin braids on the top of his head that merged into a thick braid that fell down his back. The braid was claimed to be sacred, worn by brave soldiers from Metra during King Wern's rebellion in 1148. The lit fireplace reflected in his hazel eyes and nose ring. He was quiet when we walked out the door.

I followed Da to the lake by the forest's edge—Lake Vur. He had a satchel over his shoulder, whatever trinkets were inside clattering with his every step. There was no long sentimental conversation between us, just our footsteps trudging across the muddy ground.

The moon was on display over the waters of the wide lake. When I was younger, I'd sit on the shore, thinking about swimming across one day. But the lake was so wide, the line of pine trees on the other side looked like needles.

Da stepped into the water, stopping once his feet were submerged. He reached into the satchel and removed a flask with a pointy beak. He poured a white liquid in the palm of his hand: bitterlie milk. Its source was a wildflower only found in the southwest corners of Thestlen, in the woods near our village of Heedeon. Often, it felt as if we lived isolated from the rest of the world, though Metranian laws ruled our village. But even if small, Heedeon held gems like bitterlie milk and a massive population of horned rabbits that sometimes drew hunters from the far corners of the east.

" 'Goodbye to the boy you once were.'" He waved me closer. I obliged, shuddering at the cold waters. " 'Greetings to the man you now become. With the eternal and the mortal, you are now one.'"

" 'And I now receive,'" I said, hoping to remember the poem. " 'The blessings of old and the curse from the deep. So I may ride forth one day and bring glory to my name.'" I let out a sigh of relief once I finished.

I bent down, and he smeared the cold liquid on the sides of my head before pulling a knife from his satchel.

"Your soul no longer belongs to a boy," he continued. The feeling of the cold blade against my scalp was bittersweet. Shaving the sides of my head symbolized the parts of the old me that had to be left behind. "Your breath now belongs to a man. May Hanell's holy feathers cover you. May his hands guide you." Da released a shuddering breath, as if scared of his next words. "And may his justice measure you."

Dawn crawled across the sky as my hair fell into the water. He tapped me on the shoulder when he was done.

"Happy Blood-date, Bellwound," he said with a proud smile.

"No cuts," I said.

"By the feather. Even I am proud of myself for that."

Though I had to keep with Metranian tradition, Da had never celebrated his Blood-date. He and Ma moved here when they found out about me. He read their stories and decided to follow their rules, but he never spoke of his past.

He led me back to the house where Ma waited by the entrance, wearing a long-sleeve dress tied at the waist by a leather belt. Her hair was the same acorn brown color as mine. She was to braid whatever was left of my hair to mimic the same braid Da had. All Heedeonian women had to learn the pattern once they bore a son.

She wanted to smile when she saw me. I knew she did. But her lips remained still, her golden eyes empty. I couldn't tell what occupied her mind, but she seemed to be struggling with something. My parents had always been private about their feelings. They'd ask me about mine, but I never once heard them share theirs with each other—or with me.

"Alright, Seaahra, he's all yours now." Da left me by the door. "I'm going to saddle the horses. I hope our trap caught food for tonight."

"Take your time, Stenan." She placed a hand on my back. "And shoes by the door, please, Bellwound. Can't have you smearing mud on the floor since we have guests coming tonight."

4

"Arnon, Uncle Pyeus, and Aunt Helga are hardly guests, Ma."

"All the more reason to keep the house clean."

I did as she asked. She then had me bring a chair from the kitchen to be placed in front of the large mirror by my fireplace. She was quiet as we walked through the house, up the stairs, and into my room.

"No big speech on how your little boy is all grown up?" I asked, setting the chair in front of the mirror. Having the sides of my head shaved was going to take some getting used to. "No big teary moment?"

"Trust me," she said, the rays of the morning sun flowing through the window. "That speech is whirling around in my head right now. I just don't have the strength to utter it aloud."

"Age is just a number, Ma. You taught me that."

"Mortals count years, Bellwound. Immortals count ages. Numbers aside, this is a new age for you. Your life is now split and marked by this date. Now sit down. Thank the Pale Lion your father managed to shave the sides of your head without cutting you open. That man can be so clumsy."

I smirked. "I was relieved as well."

She carefully ran her fingers through my hair, glancing at my face in the mirror. I looked more like her with my head shaved. Maybe because she always had her hair tied back. Maybe because we had the same golden eyes.

"You ever wonder why it's 'thank the Pale Lion?'" I asked. "I get that Hanell the Creator is pictured as a strong lion, but what if

Lucifer was in his right? Would it not be 'thank the Dove' then?"

She gently slapped my shoulder. "Watch your mouth, boy."

"Just thinking out loud, Ma. Stories change as they're passed down. It's very convenient to believe there is an ultimate blameless creator and an opposer. Think with me. Shadows only exist because an object blocks the light. It seems like the faith of Thestlen was written so we wouldn't think too much."

"Hold still." She held my head.

"It was just a thought," I said, noticing she didn't care for the subject.

She separated my hair into three strands. "Excited for tonight?"

"I am. Fingers crossed there's a horned rabbit or a winged fawn in the trap. Otherwise, we'll just have, what, potatoes and ale? By the dragon, Arnon wouldn't leave me alone for a year if that happened. He did trap a boar on his Blood-date."

"You and your 'by the dragon,'" she said. "'By the feather' sounds better."

"It may sound better, but dragons are more frightening than birds. And the stories of the dragon riders from Dragonfang are more interesting to me…"

My words faded away as her chin quivered and her eyes brimmed with tears. She shook her head quickly, trying to hide her sadness. She failed miserably.

"Something wrong, Ma?"

"Just thinking about life and its ages."

"You're still on that?"

"No parent is ready to see their child grow up. When they do, they finally belong to the world, and we can no longer protect them. All we can do is hope that our rights and wrongs have made them strong and ready."

"You taught me well," I said, her hands tugging at my hair.

"Trust me, Son, our teachings will soon turn to living stories in your head. And they all have twists of their own. You get to interpret them moving forward."

She spoke as if she were about to become like the fire in my hearth, a strong flame reduced to a pile of ashes.

Her hands trembled as she kept on braiding. We remained quiet until she asked me to turn around so I could inspect her work in the mirror. As I did, she ran her hand over my face, touching the scar over my left eyebrow.

"I remember when you got this," she said.

"Not easy to forget." I paused. "I hate it."

She frowned. "Scars remind us we got hurt trying."

"I disagree, Ma. They remind us we failed and lived to tell the tale." I raised a finger. "To be fair, Arnon *did* push me into the lake. Had that rock not been there, and if I hadn't passed out, I would've—"

"That's what I've always admired about you. Ever since you were a child, you've had a knack for adventure. Always so curious. So much like your father. You question everything and want to know as much as you can."

"Why are you talking like we're saying goodbye?" I grabbed her hand. "I'm just turning eighteen. I'll still be around."

"Pay no mind to your mother today." She cackled. "She's just a pile of emotions."

"Bellwound!" Da bellowed from downstairs. "Are you ready? Those horned rabbits will have decayed by the time you decide to come down."

"Coming, Da!" I shouted back, eyes still on Ma. "Are you sure you're alright?" I insisted.

"I will be." She smiled. "One day you'll marry a wonderful man, and by the grace of our Lion God, you two will have a child to raise. You'll then understand my heart now."

I kissed the top of her hand and rushed out of the house to catch up with Da.

Our horses, Oraxes and Midnight, were outside, tied to a wooden pole near the entrance. Midnight had been my mare since I was young. Her coat was dark, and her eyes were ash. Oraxes was Dad's stallion, white like the foam at the foot of a waterfall. His mane was always braided, and his scarlet eyes grew scarier with every passing year. We mounted and rode east toward the taller trees.

"Mr. Octern shared the wildest rumor this week," Da started, riding beside me. "We were at the pub and the man warned everyone that we needed to listen to him no matter how foolish he sounded."

"He's a drunk," I said. "And he managed to cheat on all four of his wives. I wouldn't trust him."

"He bothered with climbing on top of one of the tables to shout his story, Bellwound. I've never seen him do such a thing."

"All the more reason to disregard it, Da."

"He said people in the northern parts of the world have seen the dead come to life. Can you believe it?"

"Those rumors are ancient. People have always claimed they've seen the dead come to life or a diamond-eyed man or woman wander the forests at night. Tales of Nephilins and Fallen Stars and monsters."

"Every story has a hint of truth, my boy. Never disregard the tales."

"You're going to tell me you believe these rumors?" The trees rustled in the wind. "Soon, you'll be telling me you believe animals talk and mermaids swim in the far seas."

"A little faith in the Creator would do you some good," Da said.

"I don't know that it would. Not in these stories anyway. A pale lion casting out a six-winged man? The mermaids seem more believable. Maybe I'd have more faith if I could wander beyond these lands. If the stories are true, there must be evidence somewhere. Hard evidence. Something more than a book or scrolls. Something we can touch. But there aren't any here in Heedeon. Ever thought about wandering beyond the Hills of Yrthran and the River Pentan again?"

"Wanting something isn't the same as pursuing it."

"Before we left, Ma said she admired my spirit of adventure and curiosity. That I had taken after you." My words triggered a frown from him as he tightened his grasp around the reins. "When did you find peace with staying put?"

He gave the question some consideration. I thought his silence hinted that I'd made him uncomfortable, but a smile eventually crossed his lips. "After you were born," he replied. "Things change when you have a child. You'll know that someday."

The tall pines and the cornelias crowded with golden leaves marked the entrance to the forest. We had marked our path to the trap's location with a glistening golden string.

"By the feather," Da said proudly. There were five horned rabbits under the wooden crate. We had used wild purple carrots to catch them, each one infused with dragonbane so they would drift into a deep sleep. Scare a horned rabbit and the meat would be as hard as the bark of a cornelia tree.

"Five." Da alighted from Oraxes and knelt by the crate. "Five…"

"Plenty, no?" I joined him at the trap.

"Yes, plenty. Some say the number five points to the beginning of a new journey."

"Some or you?" I chuckled.

"Alright, boy. Let's get these back to the house before they wake."

Da had brought a few burlap sacks on Oraxes. We tucked the horned rabbits inside, tied them shut, and tossed them on the back of our horses—three with him and two with me.

"Did you ever hunt with O'Da?" I asked once we were on our

way. "When you lived on the other side of the River Pentan?"

"Not much to tell," he said. "Barely remember anything."

"Was he the one who told you that number five story?" I insisted.

"Maybe. I don't really remember, Bellwound."

"You never do."

There was an edge in his voice. "Some things are better left forgotten."

"How come you and Ma never talk about anyone else in our family? I know nothing about my O'Mas and O'Das. Do you have siblings? Do I have—"

"We're each other's family. The ones who truly matter."

"Did something happen back then? I can handle the truth, Da."

"That's one of the most misquoted sayings out there. You don't handle the truth. You live it."

"Arnon's parents don't talk about his relatives either," I said. "Did something happen between all of you?"

"Son, this is the only truth you need." He brought Oraxes to a halt with a pull of his reins. I stopped beside him. "There's a reason for our silence. Respect it. Honor it. Innocence is more valuable than truth."

CHAPTER TWO

I didn't push him any further. The wounds inside my da's heart had probably festered to the point beyond healing. Same with my ma.

Though Heedeonians weren't welcoming of new folk, they didn't turn them away. As the years had passed, my parents became one with this village. Every custom became theirs. They learned the food, the trades, the songs, and the stories.

I hadn't known any other life. I had never even ventured west to the city of Metra. Heedeon had been built in their territory, yet I had never gone there. People claimed rainbows covered its walls and its buildings were so high, they disappeared into the clouds.

We rode to the stable at the back of the house. Chains and knives and rope hung from the walls. In the far back was a carriage Da kept under a thick cloth. I had a vague memory of riding it when I was young.

Once Oraxes and Midnight were inside their stalls, Da meandered to one of the piles of hay. He knelt and reached behind the tangled mess.

"Lose something?"

"Ah." He smiled, revealing a dagger with a midnight hilt. "This is for you." He unsheathed it from the scabbard, its blade white like marble.

"For me?"

"The blade is dragonfang." He handed it to me, and I studied the thin vines that had been etched into the weapon.

"Where did you get this?" My face reflected on the blade's smooth surface.

"Oree. A merchant had it brought in from Winghorn months ago. I've been saving it until now. I figured it'd be the perfect opportunity for you to use it. We have five horned rabbits to skin after all."

"Thank you," I said.

He grabbed some rope and walked out of the stable. I followed him to what I called the skinner. It was nothing special, just two pieces of wood placed side by side with warping branches. I tied one of the horned rabbits by the legs so it hung facedown.

The horned rabbit's chest was still slowly rising and falling. I placed my hand behind its horns and plunged my new dagger through its skull, stabbing downward through the soft spot behind the lower jaw. I didn't want to risk missing its small heart by stabbing the chest. I cut a ring around each leg, just above the joint, and a line jutting from the rings to the backside of its gray coat. A few cuts in and the hide was ready to be peeled off.

Da observed me, but his mind was somewhere else. He looked at me as if this was going to be the last time we'd see each other.

I needed to ask Arnon if his parents had behaved the same way on his Blood-date.

I repeated the steps four more times and washed the blade in the nearby stream before walking home. Da and I brought our game to the long wooden table in the kitchen.

"This has got to be a good sign," Ma said, her hair tied in a bun.

"Since when is the number five a good sign?" Da asked with a frown, leaning on the edge of our dinner table.

"You and your stories, Stenan." Ma gently slapped his arm. "Bellwound, if you want to freshen up, I heated water for a bath."

"I won't say no to a bath after skinning those." I cocked my head toward the animals. "My hands smell like shi—"

"Ah, ah." Ma held up a finger. "You better not finish that sentence."

I walked up the stairs and into my room. The water in the round copper tub was steaming. I barred the door, got out of my dirty clothes, and sank inside.

It'd take a while for the horned rabbits to be fully cooked, but Arnon's family would probably show up before dinner was ready. They were always early.

I glanced out the window, watching the last of the yellowed leaves bounce in the wind as gray clouds hid the sun.

I'd be lying if I told my parents I wasn't planning on venturing out into the world at some point in the future. But all great adventures began with small steps. If I were to have faith in anything, it would be in the courage to take a chance. That's what fascinated me about the tale of the Pale Lion and the Dove. Lucifer took a chance and discovered something new—even if wicked. He was cast out of his home for it, but he followed his heart.

Who knew how truthful the tales were? Stories took on a life of their own whenever they were passed down. To the first storyteller, something was yellow and bright, but to the last listener, the very same thing was orange and dull.

That's why I couldn't believe in what the tales prophesied. Lucifer's return. Hanell, the Creator and Pale Lion, roaming Thestlen in the flesh. The dead coming back to life. Kingdoms had been built and destroyed because of that story. It had gathered followers who believed in its different versions. It had killed so many while providing thrones for very few.

There was something chilling about that thought—a story so powerful thousands were led to commit crimes they believed to be works of good.

I dozed off, watching the swaying branches and the colors that clung to them. It was the smell of the cooking rabbits that woke me up. By that time, the leaves had fallen from the crooked branches and the water had turned cold, shriveling my fingertips.

I remained in the bath for a while longer, thinking about the fallen leaves. Someone would only know of their existence if I shared it with them. Otherwise, they'd fade away with my memories.

And so many of my memories featured Arnon. He had always been in my life. The thought of seeing him brought on a hint of excitement. Though there was a time my feelings for him had gotten out of control, I learned to rein them in so I could keep him around.

He had never shown any interest in me beyond friendship and brotherhood. Fuck, I had seen him with the prettiest of girls at the pub. But a heart has no owner. It's a beast that obeys when it wants and awakens whenever it likes.

Whatever I had felt for Arnon before had disappeared like the autumn leaves. I didn't know if such feelings would bloom again in the future. But for now, I was content with our friendship.

Ma had brought me some blue robes from Oree a few days ago. The laced shirt was a shade brighter than the pants. A golden pattern were sewn on the shirt's hem and sleeves. The pants were meant to be tucked into boots, but not just any pair would do. Ma insisted I wear the black boots she brought home from the market last week. They were no different from the ones I already owned, aside from a few mud stains and tears on the shaft.

The Helvugs arrived early as I had predicted. Arnon hated it when I called them that. He claimed they weren't fancy enough to be bundled up as a single unit.

I couldn't remember a time when I hadn't known them. There was a strong bond between our parents, a friendship that started years before we were around. You knew they had a lot of shared experiences by the way they talked and smiled at each other.

Mr. Helvug taught the both of us to read and add numbers when we were younger. Mrs. Helvug sewed my clothes back to health when I decided to be adventurous with Arnon. They were Uncle Pyeus and Aunt Helga. But oddly, Arnon never felt like that kind of family.

Arnon and I had countless stories. From stealing crops when we were six to getting lost in the woods while searching for berries, we shared everything with each other. Though we played with the other boys and girls, we preferred each other's company.

He knew my secrets, except the ones that involved him naked in my bed. I had been able to tame the feelings, but not the intrusive fantasies. Unprovoked, they'd barge in without warning, disrupting the innocence of my mind with their tempting invitation.

He was the first person I told about Meorn, the boy who lived a few houses down. He was my first kiss. And my first everything else. And he told me all about Suella, the butcher's daughter. She was his first.

"So, Bellwound," Arnon said as I grabbed some of the chips from the bowl Ma had put out on the table. "Who'd you pay to kill those beauties for you?"

"You're confusing me with you," I said. "Remember your Blood-date? I think you hired poor old Mr. Octern to kill that elk."

"Don't be jealous that I was able to pay him." He smirked.

The thoughts were back. How could I keep them at bay when he flashed me those dimples and looked at me with those gray eyes?

"Did you also pay him to braid your hair, you fool?" I sniggered, trying to push the thoughts away.

"You're jealous of my talents." He ran his hand over the black braid falling down his back.

"Don't start," Uncle Pyeus said.

"I swear," Dad started. "If I have to break up another fight between you two."

"You know we're always horsing around, right?" Arnon said.

"Oh, and I suppose that's the excuse you used when you broke Seaahra's vase?" Aunt Helga asked. "You were both horsing around?"

"Helga," Ma said. "I hated that vase anyway. It's alright."

"And to think that years ago," Mr. Helvug said snidely. "It was just the four of us."

"Times were different then," Ma said. "It was another age."

"Never thought we'd make it this far," Da said.

"Were we that terrible when we were young?" Arnon laughed. "By the dragon…"

Ma shook her head. "You and Bellwound with 'by the dragon.'"

"It sounds more menacing," Arnon said.

We all shared a laugh. There was no heavy conversation for the rest of the night. We all ate and drank and shared stories. Da sang a few songs. He and Mr. Helvug were masters at singing. They laughed as they recalled songs from their youth, but there was one that left a deep silence after they finished.

A glory once foretold

Has brought a curse of old

From the Sea of Glass to the Mountains of Bhorn

Merry were the songs before feathers turned to flames

Foolish were the men who believed we had all been made the same

For crowns reminded us that blood spoke louder than blame

He wandered the halls of white

Humming songs into the night

Until with wine he was shamed

Forever cast out into flame

CHAPTER THREE

I stood in the doorway of their bedroom for what felt like an eternity. Whenever I was nervous, I'd sink the nail of my thumb into the pad of my fingers to ensure I wasn't dreaming. This was definitely no dream. The bloodstains on the floor were real. They led to the front door. Handprints, long streaks—signs of struggle and pain.

The rain struck the glass on the windows, my heart beating to the same uneven pace. My parents were nowhere to be seen. Their bed was broken. Their sheets were torn and scarlet stained.

How could I have slept through whatever happened? They were whisked away in the dead of night, hurt and bleeding, and I had neither heard nor seen a thing.

Why were they taken? Who would want to harm them? When did they get into the house?

I'd heard that when confronted with the unexpected, our minds try to find ways to cling to the most logical explanation. I thought about the things they said and the things they avoided saying.

Maybe a distant relative wanted them gone? Maybe they had moved to Heedeon because of a crime they committed? I tried to find a logical explanation to anchor me, but there was none.

A thud against the door sounded. I stood still, hoping it had been a branch or an animal.

Another knock, louder this time. "Bellwound, you in there?" Arnon's muffled voice boomed from the other side. "Uncle Stenan? Aunt Seaahra? Anybody?"

He stepped inside as soon as I unbolted the door, drenched. The hem of his coat and boots were stained with mud. His braid was wet and dripping. His gray eyes filled with despair.

"Something happened. Something is wrong. Something is very wrong…" His words drifted into silence as he scanned the blood-stains on the floor. "By the dragon. What happened here?"

"I'm not sure." He followed me into the wrecked bedroom, his face paling at the sight of the destruction.

"So it wasn't just my house. No, no, no—"

"What?" I asked. "Spill, damn it."

"A strange dream woke me up this morning, and I went down-stairs. Everything was quiet. But my parents' bedroom door was slightly open." He shuddered. "I peeked inside, thinking they were asleep. The room was destroyed. Blood everywhere. I checked the stable and the horses were gone." Arnon paced around, gaze fixed on the broken bed. "And I didn't hear anything. It was like I wasn't even home."

"I never woke up either," I said. "Fuck, I keep trying to find a clue. Something that could point to what happened, but there's nothing."

"Did anything happen after we left yesterday?" he asked.

"Nothing out of the ordinary. We went to bed. That was it."

"You think they're—"

"Don't say it," I demanded.

"There's fucking blood on the floor, Bellwound."

"They could just be hurt. We need to look for them. Maybe Oree? It's the closest town with Metranian guards."

Arnon rushed to the settee by the window and sat on its edge. "Those guards never bother coming here now, do they?" The water dripping from his clothes created a small puddle on the floor.

"Because nothing *ever* happens here," I said. "Until now."

He shook his head in frustration. "You're right. Oree is our best option." He pressed the heels of his hands over his eyes. "Shit. And we know every person in this village. What if the culprit lives here?"

"Let's hope you're wrong," I said.

"Your horses in the back?"

"I pray to any god they are."

I ran up to my room, put on the boots I wore at dinner yesterday, a hooded brown coat stained with mud from my ride days before, and my bear pelt before grabbing the dagger Da gave me. I glanced at the mirror on my wall before heading out. There were no bruises on my face. No signs of violence or resistance. I revisited every conversation I had with my parents yesterday. They'd acted grim, but nothing explained this.

I returned downstairs and headed out the door, Arnon at my heels. The rain struck hard. The wind was cold.

"You mentioned a dream," I said, beckoning him to rush his pace with a wave. "What was it about?"

"There was a cliff!" He walked beside me, eyes squinted, arms folded tightly over his chest. "I couldn't see the bottom. The sky was pitch black and the moon was small. I was standing at the edge, staring into nothing, when a voice called my name." He wiped the water off his face with a wrist. "I fell down the cliff and into the darkness. But then there was light. It was small at first, like a firefly. Then it grew bigger and bigger, taking the shape of a winged man. I felt strange when I woke up. Like something was moving inside me."

"Maybe you just needed to take a shit?" I asked, trying to break some of the tension. "You did eat a lot yesterday."

"Maybe." He tried to give me a smile, but it was full of worry.

I leaned against the damp brick wall of the stable to keep my balance while I trudged through the muddy soil. The lingering fog hid the east valley and the wooden houses perched amidst the trees.

The hayloft was to my left. And so was the carnage. It was like we'd walked into a butcher's shop, with the remains of Oraxes and Midnight strewn about the stable.

"Fuck," Arnon mumbled.

My feet followed the quick pace of my heart as I tried to think of a culprit. But no neighbor despised us this much. Whoever it was hadn't used a sharp blade. Their skin was raw and jagged, as if they'd been torn apart.

"Bellwound." Arnon grabbed my arm. "Look." I followed his pointed finger.

All my thoughts ground to a halt. A cloaked rider on a pitch-black horse stood by the trees. He remained frozen, perhaps expecting us to approach. Or maybe he watched us because we were next. The horse's eyes were a glimmer of light surrounded by spiked armor. The rider's drenched cloak hid his body—including his face. Three tall spikes jutted from his spaulders. And I didn't miss the sword clinging to his belt.

"What do we do?" Arnon whispered.

We couldn't run. The rider's horse was surely faster than us. So, I did the next best thing I could think of.

"Can we help you?" My voice carried through the storm, and my hand rested on the dagger at my waist.

The horse grunted and swung its neck, but the rider said nothing, his breath steaming from under his hood.

"You need something?" Arnon asked.

"Apologies," said the rider in a deep, raspy voice. "I was lost in thought. I can't quite believe I've found you both." He said every word as if in awe. "It's been years since I've been around."

"Not from here?" I asked.

"Oh, no, no," the rider replied behind a chuckle. "Definitely not."

I had to ask, even though I already knew the answer. "You did this?"

"I just want to talk. I had to ensure you would stick around."

Rage shot down my body. "You could've knocked!"

"Unfortunately, I could not."

"And our parents?" I asked.

Silence lingered.

"What do you want?" Arnon asked.

"A conversation," the rider replied.

"You expect to have a conversation after this?" I retorted.

"Invite me into your home, Bellwound." His horse snorted as he pulled on the reins.

All of a sudden, my knees felt weak. "How do you know my name?"

"I've gone through shadow and flame to find you," said the rider. "The Fallen Stars know your names. We've been waiting for your Blood-date since the Age of the Regent."

"You waited five thousand years?" I asked, confused.

"The Fallen Stars are patient," he said.

"The Fallen…" I repeated. "As in…"

"The servants of Lucifer, our Dove." He wheezed. "I'm sure you've heard of us. Thestlen is rich in tales about our kind. Some are right. Most are wrong."

Coincidence? Maybe. Maybe not. The things Da said, Ma's conversation as she braided my hair, the song, and now this—a Fallen Star in our village.

I clung to the lingering silence until the rider pierced it. "I'm trying to be patient." The ghostly horse marched forward. "My orders are to have a conversation with you. I want to be faithful to the orders I was given." He hesitated as if he were about to utter blasphemy. "Please."

A scream. Arnon. No blade pierced him. Nothing in sight caused him pain, but his legs failed him. He plunged to his knees, hands curling into fists, before collapsing on the ground. He started writhing, rolling in the mud like an animal.

"Arnon!" I knelt beside him and pinned his shoulders to the ground. Mud splattered over his face as his body shook. "Arnon, what—what's going on?"

"She did her job after all," said the rider. "The seed is inside him." He alighted from his armored beast. "The hosts are ready in the Dark Beyond. They're ready to cross over."

"What's inside him?"

His feet sank into the ground. He removed the cloak from his face, revealing fair hair and red eyes that glistened in the dark.

"Scarlet eyes…" I whispered to myself before calling out to him. "What do you want?"

"I've told you what I want. A conversation. Do as you're told and Arnon's suffering will cease. You have something of great value. I must show you what's beneath your home. Come with me and your friend's pain will stop."

Arnon mumbled something inaudible as his face paled. I tried reading his purple lips, but I couldn't understand his plea.

"Seaahra and Stenan raised a stubborn idiot," the rider said with a nod. "I'll tell you that."

"How do you know my parents?"

He chuckled as he stepped forward. "You ask a lot of questions, boy."

Arnon gasped for air. His eyes begged me for help. His suffering was stronger than my fear. "Fine, fine. I'll take you there. I'll do whatever you want. Please stop. Make it stop."

Arnon's suffering ceased with a snap of the rider's fingers. He swallowed a long breath, holding a hand around his throat.

"My name is Crocell," he said proudly while Arnon coughed and gagged. "The first Fallen Star to find its host in this new age. The Age of the Fallen. Now, shall we—"

A distant gallop and neigh pierced the storm. Crocell's gaze followed the sound coming from the trees. A rider on a white horse appeared. The approaching man unsheathed his sword, holding it forward. Crocell followed suit, raising a blade gray as ash with chipped edges.

The rider's golden hair was tied into a bun, a few wisps falling over his eyes. Their blue was no match for the storm. He stood up in the saddle, clutching his horse's ashen mane and using one knee for balance.

Crocell tapped his horse's neck, the animal fleeing into the woods, leaving him on foot. He held out his arms, ready for whatever fate came at him.

The man on the white horse took to the air, leaping at a height impossible for a human. Crocell darted upward while the man used a tree as a platform to lunge his body toward his opponent. I couldn't keep up with their movements. The raindrops struck their bodies as they attacked each other in midair, in the trees, and on the ground.

"Can you run?" I asked Arnon as the fight continued.

"I think so," he said.

We didn't look back. I pressed my thumb nail into the pads of every single finger, wishing this was a nightmare. "Wake up, wake up," I mumbled as we ran across the short misty distance between the stable and my house. But this was no dream.

I wasn't sure of many things, but there was one truth that anchored me as we approached my doorstep. Death had come for me and my family.

CHAPTER FOUR

I bolted the door shut. Arnon collapsed onto the settee, still gasping for air.

"Are you alright?" I knelt in front of him. "Talk to me."

"Yes." He struggled to get the words out. "I'm fine." He coughed. "That man—"

"Shh," I said. "Rest your voice. And that was no fucking man."

"Rest?" He cleared his throat, finding his voice and getting louder. "Fuck resting. Who was he?" He sat up with a sudden bewildered clarity. "Do you think Crocell took our parents?"

"I don't think so," I replied. "He can't get in here without consent for some reason. It couldn't have been him."

"And who was that other—" A pounding on the door stole his words.

"Open up!" a voice shouted. "Bellwound! Arnon! I'm no enemy!"

"He knows our names," Arnon whispered. "How?"

A loud thud. Hinges flitted across the room as the door plummeted to the ground.

"We need to leave." The man with the diamond eyes rushed inside, unscathed from his fight. "Grab a couple of things you might need and let's go."

"What do you mean *let's go*?" I shouted. Drenched from the rain, the man paced around the house, leaving mud trails on the floor. His clothes were too fancy to be worn in a storm. Maybe he'd been in a rush to get here. The collar of his dark blue gambeson rose near his jawline. Gold thread had been used to sew a symbol into the fabric, a circle with a square and a triangle in the middle. Between them was another circle with a cross. He showed no signs of being weary from his fight.

"Why are you not getting ready?" he asked. "Have you already forgotten that abomination we crossed paths with?"

"I didn't forget him," I said. "But I know he can't get in here without an invitation. I don't know you."

"Right now,"—he stabbed his finger toward me—"the only thing you need to be concerned with is gathering food and supplies. We're going away and, trust me, we have no idea if or when you'll be coming back here. Hurry up. My horse is outside alone in the rain."

"I don't give a damn about your horse."

"Is Crocell dead?" Arnon asked.

"*Dead?*" He shook his head. "Your parents have taught you nothing. They insisted on keeping the two of you in the dark." His hands pressed on his hips. "Crocell is a Fallen Star and can't die. Well, not yet, anyway. They may be wounded due to the mortality of their human host, but die? Not yet…" He continued to stalk around the house, clearly on the hunt.

"Lose something?" I asked.

"I'll lose my patience if you don't pack," he said with an edge. "Just do as I say. I will explain everything."

Arnon and I shared a look of concern. What other choice did we have? Who was to say this man wouldn't kill us if we didn't comply?

I rushed to the kitchen, Arnon at my heels. I grabbed one of the burlap sacks and filled it with bread and fruit. Waking up today, I never imagined this would be the last time I'd see my house for a while.

A sudden loud bang drew me back to the common area. The man was tearing the wooden floor apart with his bare hands.

"What the fuck are you doing?" I asked, stunned.

"Looking for the thing Crocell wanted so badly." His attention remained on the expanding hole.

"Looking for— What's *your* name?" I demanded.

"Oriah."

"What are you?" I asked.

He let out a frustrated sigh. "To say that you shouldn't fear my kind would be foolish. But you don't have to be afraid of who I am now. I'm on your side. Now as for what I am—"

"Nephilin," Arnon said.

"Smart boy…" He trailed off, in awe of whatever he had found beneath my floor. He wiped his brow with a wrist, his expression turning somber. "Here it is." He pulled out a rusty silver box from the debris.

He wiped the thick coat of dust from its surface, revealing a symbol set dead center, a winged crown with three wings on the right and three on the left.

"And what is that exactly?" My heart pounded.

His fingers traced the symbol. "The Mezar." He tucked the box inside the satchel around his shoulder. "It houses Lucifer's epistle. Do you have a carriage around? Your parents used to have one."

"It's out back, but wait, so there's a letter inside—"

He opened the door. His white horse stood outside, unbothered by the storm.

"Off we go," he said.

I glanced around the house until my gaze met Arnon's frightened stare.

"Crocell may not enter your house without an invitation, Bellwound," Oriah said. "But knowing his kind, he will kill every person in this village until you agree to let him in. We need to leave. I promise to tell you everything on the way."

"The stories are true," Arnon said. "Aren't they? Hanell the Creator and the Dove and the Stars and the Fallen Stars. All of it."

"Some of it," he replied. "Others are fables inspired by truth. I *need* you to come with me. We have much to do."

I reluctantly left my home behind. Arnon walked alongside me,

Oriah stalked behind us, and his horse followed.

I led them to the stable. The cold rain struck my skin, sending shivers down my body as we trod across the muddy ground. We walked past my dead horses. I avoided looking at them.

Everything appeared the same as it did yesterday. There was still a pile of hay in the corner. The feeder still sat beside an empty bucket. The carriage was still in the back, covered by a thick cloth.

I grabbed the hilt of the dagger at my waist. When I received it yesterday, I could have never dreamt this nightmare would unfold the next morning.

"Perfect," whispered Oriah.

The hanging chains rattled at the clash of thunder. A cloud of dust lifted into the air as he uncovered the two-wheeler.

"It's going to be a bit tight," Oriah said. "But it'll do."

"Where are we going?" Arnon asked.

His horse strolled inside, standing in front of the carriage. Oriah twirled a finger in the air. The horse obeyed the movement, turning around.

"He asked you a question," I insisted.

Oriah ignored me.

"If you expect us to get on that carriage, you better start giving us some answers," I demanded.

He remained quiet while saddling the horse.

"What the fuck did you mean by Lucifer's epistle? Is there a letter inside that box?" He climbed atop the carriage, ignoring every word spilling out of my mouth.

"How did this Mezar box end up in Bellwound's house?" Arnon asked.

"By everything that's pure and cursed," he snapped. "You two don't understand how dire your situation is. We can stay here, chat, and get caught by one of the Fallen Stars again, or we can be on our way, and I'll explain everything while we're on the road."

"You don't fucking get it." I stabbed a finger at him. "Our parents are gone. You showed up out of nowhere, broke down my door, tore my house apart, dug up a box that belongs to good old Lucifer, and you expect us to trust you?"

"I save you from being snatched by a Fallen Star and you think you should fear me?" He scoffed. "You're Bellwound Throvar. Son of Seaahra and Stenan Throvar. Born on the fiftieth day of autumn in the year thirteen ten. I knew about the Mezar because of my bond with your parents. I know your past. I know where you both come from." He shifted his gaze to Arnon. "And you, Arnon Helvug. I'm no stranger to your parents either."

"You can give us answers?" I asked.

"Many," he replied. "On the way!"

Instinctively, Arnon and I locked eyes before our legs simultaneously carried us forward. We climbed up and sat beside him. With a whistle, the horse carried us out of the stable.

Oriah muttered under his breath, "Perhaps you not only need a savior, but a sitter as well."

The rain had stopped. It didn't take long for the little hilltop homes to be replaced by dense forest. The storm had doomed most of the autumn leaves to the ground. After a while, Heedeon was no longer within sight. We headed northeast, toward the Fields of Mehnor.

"Where are we going?" I asked, shivering as the deluge returned.

"To meet the Council," he responded. "And to hopefully get you some warm clothes."

"Oh, the Council!" I slapped Arnon's shoulder. "You know, the Council, the people we've never heard of. We're going there!"

Oriah refrained from speaking. Neither Arnon nor I dared to pierce the quiet.

The area was familiar to Arnon and me. Our families would fish in the little rivers and pick apples and berries from the trees. We'd also camp out here when we had the time.

Hours went by. We stopped in a clearing at dusk and resorted to the fruits I had brought since the bread was soggy from the rain.

"At least you have heard of Hanell and Lucifer," Oriah blurted, resting his shoulder on the side of the carriage.

"What, all you needed was food to talk?" I asked with an apple in hand, sitting on a rock.

"Food and patience," he replied under a breath.

"We know the story," Arnon said. "My dad taught us. The immortal beings who lived in Valleyner."

"Lucifer, the Dove, was cast out of Valleyner because of his rebellion." I scoffed. "Honestly, I never believed the stories. There's so much that didn't make sense. And the heavy prophecies. 'The doom of Thestlen will come—'"

"'When the Dove returns for blood,'" Oriah finished.

"We know enough," I said. "But this rusty box—"

"The Mezar," Oriah interrupted. "Call it by its name."

"The Mezar," I continued, cocking my head toward his waist. "According to you, there's an epistle inside it. But what's so threatening about some scrawled words that Lucifer would send a Fallen Star to retrieve it?"

"There's power in words written in secret," Oriah said. "No one in this mortal realm or in the realm of the gods knows what's written in this epistle. We knew that, when the time came, a mortal would point to its location. But not only did you show the Fallen Stars the location of the Mezar, but your Blood-date also set Lucifer's spirit free once more."

The apple fell from my suddenly numb hand.

"Nothing can conceal a living spirit once it's freed," he continued.

"Why me?" I asked.

"I've been asking myself the same question," he said. "The Council heard the Mezar's call. It led me here. To your house. To you." His teeth sank into the apple in his hand. "Crocell was the first Fallen Star to return. But he didn't return to his own body. The man you saw, that's not him. That was a human being used as a host for the Fallen Star's spirit. Judging by his armor, we can assume they have a base somewhere in Thestlen already. That was no human armor."

"So the dead are coming back to life," I said. "The Shadows, they are real as well?"

"I wouldn't call it *life*. I'd call it control," Oriah said. "For a long while, the spirits of those who passed found rest. But not anymore. Not since yesterday."

"Have you seen one?" Arnon asked.

"Not yet." Oriah's face went cold. "But it's only a matter of time until the living does."

CHAPTER FIVE

The forest lay quiet under the light of a full moon. Arnon suggested we build a fire, but Oriah warned that we should lay low until reaching the borderline—whatever that meant.

Oriah freed his horse from the carriage, tied it around a wide tree trunk, and laid down between its roots. We only had the forest floor as a bed. I found a somewhat comfortable position among a few roots and twigs several yards away. But I wasn't sure how I was supposed to sleep after the past several hours. I was still adjusting to the reality that the place I had so many pleasant memories had become a living nightmare.

Arnon lay to my left, out of reach, but not too far from my sight. He tossed and turned, hands folded over his chest—a habit he'd had since we were kids. Frustrated, he got to his feet, wiped his hands on his thighs, and walked my way.

"He said he knew of my parents." Arnon's breath was steam as he laid next to me. My heart rushed when our shoulders touched.

"Just like he knows mine," I said with a shudder.

"Lift your head." He put his arm under my neck and pulled me close, so my head rested on his chest. "Now we'll both be warm."

Whatever his intentions were, I didn't fight it.

"And no," Arnon said. "He knew *of* my parents."

"And?"

"Makes me question why he mentioned yours by name and mine in passing. That's all. Maybe I'm overthinking it."

"I don't blame you." I struggled to keep my thoughts in my head and my blood from rushing downward. The only thing I could excuse growing stiff would be my hands in this chill. He had never held me this close before, but perhaps he was just a friendly shoulder in the middle of all this chaos. "We're allowed to overthink after the day we've had."

"Stars, Fallen Stars, Lucifer," Arnon mumbled. "All the tales are true. I wonder if my dream was some kind of warning."

"How so?" I raised my head, my eyes meeting his. I begged my cock not to rise too.

"Did you forget the stories my dad used to read during our lessons?" he asked. "I know you weren't that interested in talking Faith, but still."

"Help me remember."

"A few of the books sent out by the Faith claimed Lucifer had six wings," he said, his eyes heavy with sleep. "And I dreamt of a six-winged man the night before all this…"

His eyelids closed slowly. My head returned to his shoulder.

I watched his chest rise and fall, relieved that the mystery of his dreams muted my thoughts about him.

A low melodious hum traveled through the air. It was Oriah. I slowly got to my feet so Arnon wouldn't wake and followed the humming.

"He does overthink things, doesn't he?" Oriah asked as I approached. His back was pressed against a tree, legs stretched out and crossed, fingers laced on his lap.

"At least he managed to fall asleep," I said. "Unlike us."

"Well, him and Crystal here." He pointed at his horse. One of the mare's hind legs was relaxed, the hoof resting on its toe.

"I didn't know she had a name."

"All good horses do. Crystal has gotten me through many things."

"So did mine," I said. "Before they were killed."

I sat beside him, pretending the twisted roots jutting out of the ground was a cushioned seat.

"Let me guess. More questions."

"You really need to guess?"

"I may as well answer them since I can't get a wink of sleep out here. It's hard to sleep away from her."

"Her?"

"You'll meet her. She's been by my side for thousands of years." He sighed. "But I assume your questions have nothing to do with my personal affairs."

"No," I said behind a chuckle. "No, they don't."

"So ask before I regret this conversation."

"I heard that your kind exploded into existence. Stardust, mermaid dust, even illuminated sand. I heard many stories about your kind. My parents were the ones more interested in holy books. The tales are all jumbled in my head. I've also heard of a girl—"

"Stardust." He chuckled. "Now that's a good one."

"Any of those true?"

"I wish they were." The light of the moon made it bright enough for me to notice his eyes growing distant. "Prey and predators aren't meant to fall in love. The natural order of things is for the lion to kill the sheep, the cat to hunt the dove. That's not what happened two thousand years ago, before castles and kingdoms and crowns and stories. To the east, near the Mountain of Tears, was the first village of the Conscient—the village of Cellendrane."

"The first humans with coherent thoughts."

"Correct," he said. "Their minds had developed far more than their ancestors', but they weren't aware of the predators roaming among their people. The Fallen Stars were already searching for cracks in Hanell's creation. It was an innocent man and woman who ended up being vessels for darkness. A Fallen Star found a home inside the man. He was posing as a lost traveler when he saw her. They were both taken with each other, and she bore a child within a month."

"The Fallen's?"

"Yes. Nephilins were born when the natural order of things got…"

"Fucked up," I finished.

"That's one way to put it."

"How is that possible?" I asked. "A baby in a month?"

"Cursed blood mixed with mortal blood," he said. "Lucifer already slumbered in the Dark Beyond and Fallen Stars had found a way back into this world. More Fallen Stars slept with human men and women, and the first generation of Nephilins was born. Well, the first and last. Our human parents were killed after a few years. And we were ordered to live underground. My kind is spread across this world. I am from the west, from Sandrovar."

A darkness seeped into his words. There was no pride in his account, only regret.

"How did you know where we were?" I asked. "Did the Mezar call to you?"

"You've been watched your whole life," he said, gazing at the sky. "The Council keeps an eye on you."

"You're lying."

"What?"

"If that were true, my parents wouldn't have vanished," I said. "There wouldn't have been blood all over—"

"I said they keep an eye on you. Not that they intervene."

"Why wouldn't they?"

"Sometimes the people we love go down paths that don't welcome us," he replied, his face grieving a past I didn't fully know. "And we must make peace with their absence. Your parents, both of your parents, belonged to the holy Council before they left for

47

Heedeon. Some decisions were too costly for them. Well, for all of us. I promised to do my part by you. And here I am."

"Did they ever regret leaving?" I asked.

The night couldn't hide Oriah's glistening eyes. "Sleep is finally catching up to me." He quickly got to his feet. "You take this spot. I'll find someplace else to rest."

He meandered through the trees, disappearing after a moment. Crystal remained still. And I struggled to find a position on the forest floor where there wasn't a rock poking at my back or a root nudging me to leave.

My stubborn mind wanted to stay awake until sunrise, but my body was tired. Through the swaying branches, I could make out a few scattered stars. But it was the two bright spots lingering in the shadows that held my attention. Crystal neighed loudly, her neck jolting up. She paced back and forth, trying to break free.

I narrowed my eyes, and the two white spots rushed right. Branches rustled above me. A foul stench suddenly filled the air. The bright circles were getting bigger, closer.

I heard something creeping across the forest floor and I quickly sat up. But it was only Oriah. He held a finger over his lips, signaling that I should remain quiet as he neared.

I looked back up to see the two bright circles sway upward before plunging to the ground. A thud. And then it walked out of the vegetation. It was shaped like a man and smelled like a mix of horse shit and rotten meat. The faint light of the moon brushed its mangled face. It had holes where its eyes should have been and tattered lips that revealed its teeth.

It trudged forward, curious. It walked past Crystal, heading in Arnon's direction—who somehow remained asleep.

I knew what it was. The story Da heard at the pub was true. The dead had returned.

Oriah grasped the hilt of his sword. My fingers gripped the dagger at my waist.

Crystal stomped, neighing as if in pain. Arnon didn't wake. Oriah's eyes begged me to remain still, but I wasn't sure how long I could comply.

My fingers clawed at the dirt as the creature wheezed. It stood in front of Arnon, waiting. It stretched its skeletal hand, reaching for Arnon's face.

I had already lost so much. I wasn't going to lose him. My hold around the dagger tightened. I wished for any skill I had with a blade to take over. I unsheathed the weapon and threw it, barely aiming, hoping it'd strike any part of its body. It missed my target, striking a tree instead.

The creature's head jerked my way. Its howling screech numbed me with fear.

Arnon's eyes shot open. Once he realized what stood in front of him, he tripped the Shadow with his leg and rolled away on the ground.

Oriah leapt into the air and landed on top of the creature with his sword in hand. The blade reflected the light of the moon as it pierced the Shadow's chest and its body exploded into ash.

Arnon got to his feet. "What the fuck was that?"

"A Shadow," I said, retrieving my weapon lodged in the tree trunk. "Right?"

"Yes." Oriah tried to hide the fear in his voice, searching the trees.

Breaking twigs and heavy footsteps sounded first from my right, then from my left. More bright spots appeared, and it was as if the entire forest was crowded with stars.

"Go right. I'll go left," Oriah said. "I'll find you. Go!"

Oriah darted into the trees.

Arnon and I ran.

A loud squeal echoed behind me. I chanced a look over my shoulder. One of those things was on top of Crystal, tearing her open like she was paper.

The sight gave me a burst of speed. We leapt over fallen trees, trampling anything in our path. The light of the moon reflected on a river cutting through the landscape with its strong current. If judgment served me right, it was the River Yund.

"What now?" Arnon's breath steamed as he placed his hands on his knees.

"We swim across." I tried to measure the distance to the other side. "That's the only way."

"Across? We'll freeze our asses off."

Screeches pierced my ears, growing louder with every second.

"We have to try." I rushed toward the water. One foot went in, and it was cold—burning cold. A few steps and it reached my waist.

"Come on—" Something tugged at my ankle. Then everything went cold and dark. After a brief moment of confusion, I realized I had gone under.

"Bellwound!" I heard Arnon's muffled scream while being dragged to the bottom. In the water was one of the Shadows, its cat-like eyes glistening like a bright firefly. I kicked it, trying to break free, but the more I resisted, the deeper its bony fingers pulled me.

Suddenly, Oriah emerged from behind the grotesque being, piercing its skull with his blade. Its body dispersed into ashes, the remains floating upward and following the current.

I kicked toward the surface, gasping for air as soon as my head emerged. Oriah came up beside me, pulling me to shore by my sleeve. Arnon rushed my way, helping me out of the water.

Footsteps echoed amidst our shivers. Shadows appeared from the forest, their arms dangling lifelessly as they wobbled closer—an army of the dead.

A hooded figure walked ahead of them, as if wanting all to know they led the walking dead. They removed the cloak from their face. Crocell's scarlet eyes stared at me once again.

"It's a travesty that you keep protecting these boys, Oriah," he said, spreading out his hands. "You're making this a lot more difficult, you see. Helstrid won't be pleased. You may have left your kind, but you're still our child."

"I may be damned, but I can still make choices," Oriah said.

The growls got louder, the screeches a dagger in my ears. The Shadows were riled up, like leashed, starving beasts staring at their prey.

"Choose kindness, Nephilin. The seed of darkness found him a long time ago." Crocell's gaze briefly shifted to Arnon. "And Lucifer only wants to talk to Bellwound."

"Oh, do shut up." Arnon stabbed a finger at Crocell. "Just tell those fuckers to kill us. You have the numbers. Stop whatever game you're playing and be done with it already."

Crocell scoffed. "They're not here to kill you, Arnon. They're here to serve you." A smile crossed his lips. "They're chasing you because of your stubbornness. If suffering is what it takes for you lot to learn to obey, then so be it."

"So this is fun to you?" I took a determined step forward, hands clenching into fists. "Is that it?"

"Satisfying would be the better word," he said as I approached. "You, epistle-keeper, you none of us can touch. All we can do is surround you with darkness and shadow, so your purpose is clear."

He wasn't much taller than me. I was tired of being chased. I was tired of being treated like some helpless victim. He talked of purpose as if he were Da.

"You know what's also satisfying?" I asked, standing only inches from him.

"What?" he asked. His confusion was the distraction I needed. My knuckles struck his jawbone. Pain shot up my arm—my reward for punching him.

He stumbled back a step, holding a hand over his mouth.

"Make your death threats now," I said. "I see you bleed just like we do."

My hand throbbed from the blow. He wiped the blood from the corner of his mouth, staring at the hint of scarlet on his thumb.

Flashes of light appeared around him. They twisted into each other, like a braid. The light faded away to reveal dark feathers. A pair of wings had materialized. "I have orders not to kill you," he said, the muscles on his face trembling. "But I could break my promise, come up with an excuse, and have you wander the Dark Beyond."

"What would happen to you then?" Arnon stepped closer. "They'd torture you, huh? Maybe tear you apart? It's clear that you can still die in that mortal body. Then you'd be sent back to the darkness you lingered in for so long."

Anger flooded Crocell's scarlet eyes. They pierced Oriah as if trying to tear him open. "Fucking Nephilin," he said through gritted teeth. "I hope our Dove has his way with you when you come around. Or perhaps he'll have his way with her. You know he's not picky when it comes to that."

The veins in Oriah's neck bulged. His chin quivered as rage took over.

"Maybe he'll make her his little bitch," Crocell continued.

Oriah remained still, but his eyes showed the storm that raged inside him.

Crocell turned and walked away, retreating into the forest. The Shadows followed, limping and squalling as their feet trampled over branches and twigs.

My chest rushed up and down, my hand throbbing with my every breath.

"Oriah, what does he mean by the seed of darkness?" Arnon asked. "I've heard it twice now."

"There's darkness inside every one of us," Oriah said, eyeing the spot where Crocell had stood after I punched him.

"And that talk of Shadows serving Arnon?" I asked. "That was a strange speech, no?"

Oriah took a hesitant breath. "Stranger than everything else you've witnessed until now?"

"Alright," I said, teeth chattering. "I get it. You don't feel like talking."

"Some things aren't my responsibility to explain," Oriah said with an edge. "You both had parents. They should've done the talking." He swallowed the rest of his speech. "Let's carry on."

"Give me the satchel," I demanded.

"What?" Oriah's eyes leapt out of their sockets.

"If I'm the epistle-keeper, then I want to carry it," I said with an outstretched hand.

"If those things come back—"

"Well, they just left." I beckoned for the satchel with a wave. "It was in my house. And according to them, it belongs to me."

"It isn't yours, Bellwound," Oriah said. "It's only yours to keep safe. If they retrieve—"

"They could've retrieved it now," I said. "But they didn't. Crocell called me the epistle-keeper. And according to him, I can't be touched. I don't think the same can be said for you."

"Bellwound is right," Arnon said. "They could've killed us and taken it. But they didn't."

Oriah frowned. "You doubt my words?"

"I doubt the stories," I replied. "It's nothing personal."

He shook his head in disbelief. I didn't care. He removed the satchel from his shoulder and dropped it on the ground. "As you wish. But we don't stop tonight. Movement will keep the two of you warm."

"Fine by me," I said.

Oriah walked ahead, following the river. I tried to stop my teeth from chattering. Arnon's was already loud enough. He was lost in thought. I didn't need to ask to know his mind lingered on what Crocell had said.

Darkness was indeed inside all creatures, but not the way Crocell had implied. What he spoke of was something else—something more. A seed of darkness that somehow forced the dead to bend the knee.

CHAPTER SIX

We traveled for two days, following the River Yund. I had never left the borders of Heedeon before. The farthest I'd ever gone was when Da took me to the village of Oree out west. But I had never seen the castles and walls of the big kingdoms.

As we walked, I thought about how I had lived my entire life near these woods but never ventured through them. The security of home had made me too comfortable to tread on new ground. Perhaps I'd also grown too comfortable with the silence surrounding my family's past. And it had now come back to haunt me.

The waters of the river reflected the blue of the midday sky, nestled between the mossy ground we stood on and a riverbank crowded with pine trees on the other side. The Mountain of Solace was in view, its snow-covered summit using the clouds as a shield.

"I can't believe we're only now seeing this for the first time," Arnon said, standing on the riverbank beside me. "We lived two days away and never bothered to come here."

"It happens to the best of us," Oriah said. "I lived underground for thousands of years. I never cared to journey through Thestlen until I started questioning my own kind. It's either curiosity or danger that sparks courage in us. Don't be sad you were deprived of this view. Find joy that you get to see it now."

Oriah led us to a set of ruins scattered by the water—columns, statues, and archways covered by the leaves of autumn. History was carved into the remains. There were horses, swords, warriors, and winged men and women. A circular stairway was still standing. Its bottom step was buried beneath the ground. Its first step stood as tall as my head, ascending into the sky, though surely it once led somewhere else. The leaves crunched beneath my feet as I strolled around the ruins, gazing at the intricate patterns carved on stone and marble.

A mist appeared over the water, crawling its way to shore, moving across the ruins with intent. Oriah was unbothered by its presence.

Arnon and I exchanged a worried glance, but as the mist thickened, his face disappeared from sight. I reached out and touched his shoulder.

"I'm still here," he said.

"Oriah?" I searched for him.

"Still here."

An eerie silence descended. The autumn leaves beneath my feet seemed to have been replaced by soft grass. And the smell. It smelled like newly blooming flowers after winter.

The mist thinned slowly, revealing branches heavy with red leaves above me. Mountain ranges came into view, stretching across the horizon, their peaks covered in snow. At their base was a forest that mirrored a colorful painting with shades of red, yellow, and orange.

I had to accept the impossible notion that the mist had taken us somewhere else. Heedeon had but one mountain near it—the Mountain of Solace. I counted and there were about seven peaks around me.

The mist crawled away, hovering behind me as if respecting some invisible barrier. The tall statue of a white six-winged lion perched between the trees. My head only reached its chest. The animal had a peaceful look on its face. Its wings were wide, their tips curving inward as if creating a shelter for whoever stood beneath.

The trees around me seemed old, so old that if they could speak, they would probably share tales from a time before humans and crowns and epistles.

"Welcome to Heelyan, in the world of Valleyner," Oriah said. "The borderline is the only way the Gifted can get here. There are a couple of them scattered around Thestlen."

"Valleyner," I mumbled. "The realm of Hanell the Creator?"

"Correct," Oriah replied. "Heelyan is in the south of Valleyner."

"Anyone can just cross over?" Arnon gazed at the lion statue.

"Like I said, only the Gifted. People chosen by the Faith, immortals, and humans like you."

"I'm sorry," Arnon started. "But when you say Gifted, do you mean we have powers? Can we make things disappear?"

"Being Gifted simply means your purpose is beyond the ordinary," Oriah said. "Like Bellwound being the epistle-keeper and you…" he shuddered.

Arnon frowned. "And me?"

"And you being the son of Council members. They're chosen by the Faith to sit where they do."

I sensed that wasn't the answer he truly meant to share.

My mind went back to the morning of my Blood-date. Ma had talked about years and ages, and how my life was being split up by the two. Did she know? Did Da know? Did Oriah know more than he let on?

Squirrel-like critters crawled up the trees, their coats glimmering with golden dust. The light of the sun pierced the canopy, casting shadows on the forest floor.

But it wasn't the strange animals that left me speechless. The vegetation gave way to a moat around a castle of white walls. My heart beat a bit faster as my gaze followed its three towers into the sky, the middle one standing higher than the others.

"By the dragon," Arnon said. "This place… Never seen anything like it."

"Not even in your dreams?" I smirked.

We crossed the drawbridge, coming to tall iron doors. Both creaked open, but not before I caught sight of the carved patterns shaped like tangled roots.

A man rushed our way, wearing a black tunic beneath a scarlet cloak. His graying hair was wavy and parted in the middle, falling a little under his ears.

"And hea' dey ah'!" he said in a cheerful voice, spreading his arms. "All of ye made it safe. Ye're all safe."

"Had a few setbacks along the way, Atholeeon," Oriah said.

They shared a quick hug. This Atholeeon stared at Arnon and me for a few seconds before speaking to us. "Bellwound T'rovar and Arnon Helvug." He chuckled. "Ye're de spittin' image of yer parents."

"Do you know where they are?" I asked, hopeful.

He sighed. "We keep a close watch ova' Thestlen, and yet yer parents slipped t'rough our fingers. We're doing all we can to find 'em." He beckoned us closer with a wave. "But donnot lose hope. I'm sure dey're fine. Brave and strong. Now come on, come on." He clapped his hands. "Let us talk! Der's much to discuss."

"Where is she?" Oriah asked.

"In de study room," Atholeeon said with a smile.

"I'll leave them with you then," Oriah said and headed inside the castle.

I assumed this man was on our side since Oriah didn't hesitate to leave us alone with him.

I had more questions about the whereabouts of our parents, but I couldn't bring myself to speak as Arnon and I marveled at the sight beyond the entryway. White marble had been used to build the floors, and tall columns of the same color ascended to the ceiling. A glistening staircase lingered in front of us, suspended in midair. The light of the sun leaked through a glass dome above us.

Atholeeon led us into a dining room on the left of the stairs.

There was a wooden table long enough to sit twelve. Above it was an iron chandelier lit by red wax candles.

"Sit, sit, sit." Atholeeon smiled. "I'll go into de kitchen n' ask me servants to bring us food. We can chat den."

"Thanks," I said.

He left the room like a giddy child.

"He seems very happy to see us," Arnon said as he took a seat.

"Too happy, wouldn't you say?" I sat beside him, facing a fireplace.

"Loosen up, Bellwound," he said. "We're safe."

"Right," I mumbled. "Safe."

The art on the walls and ceilings depicted landscapes, rivers, and winged men and women that I assumed were Stars.

Arnon and I embraced the quiet, observing the paintings. I imagined my parents sitting in this very dining room. Ma walking through the doors, strolling down the hall with Da. Perhaps this was where they fell in love.

If the impending doom following me wasn't so present, I'd be able to appreciate the charm and beauty of the place more. My first time seeing a castle and it wasn't even of my own world. But every swirl carved into wood and every brush stroke on the walls stirred questions about an unknown and dangerous past.

Atholeeon returned with a silver tray filled with bread and roast chicken. The smell of the food turned my stomach into a beast once he set it on the table.

"I'll be back wif'—" I went for a slice of bread. Arnon grabbed a thigh "—forks an' knives…"

"It's been three days, sir," Arnon said, his mouth full of food. "Hard to wait."

"It's alright." Atholeeon sat beside me. "Eat, eat, eat! Ye deserve a good meal. We'll feast properly tonight, eh?"

"A feast?" I asked.

"I cannot simply have de children of Seaahra and Stenan T'rovar and Pyeus and Helga Helvug come to me doorstep wit'out a proper greeting.

"How'd they end up here?" Arnon asked. "When were they chosen?"

"How much d'ye know?" Atholeeon folded his hands over the table.

"Nothing," I replied. "They never told us a thing."

"Tell ye what," Atholeeon said. "Ye finish yer food. We'll go for a quick walk. I want to show ye t'ings. How does dat sound?"

"Good," I said.

I was already eating with my hands. And now curiosity was to blame for me speeding up my pace. There were answers here, and Atholeeon was willing to share them. We finished eating, washed our hands with some water that was inside a bucket by the corner, and were led out.

Atholeeon led us up the staircase suspended in midair and into a long, wide hallway. Satin curtains draped beside a window to our left, a view of the moat on the other side. The sculptures were all of winged men and women. Some clothed in robes, others naked. Canvases showing all sorts of different landscapes hung on the walls. And at the very end was a tall wooden door. Atholeeon twisted its silver knob, revealing another hall with many doors.

"Behold, de chambers of the Council members." Atholeeon held the door open.

"How many members are there now?" Arnon asked.

"Eight, if ye count me," he replied, locking the door behind us. "We were twelve until yer parents left. De Fait' hasn't recruited any new members since."

The hall paled in comparison to the rest of the castle. It was missing the statues, canvases, and curtains that were present in other rooms. Instead, the space was barren—everything, except for the dark brown doors, a pure white.

"Where were our parents recruited from?" Arnon asked.

"Metra." Atholeeon walked ahead of us. "Dese last four doors hea', dese were your parents' rooms when dey lived hea'."

"They slept in separate rooms?" I asked.

"Dey were supposed to," he answered, trying to hide his disappointment.

"Even after being together?" Arnon stepped forward, approaching the door to the left.

"None knew dey were," Atholeeon said. "And when we did, it was too late."

"Too late for what?" I asked.

"Council members are meant to be alone, ye see? 'Til the end. Now dey, dey hid deir love. Bot' of yer parents did. And den dey left."

"They just… left." I glanced at the silver knob on the door to my right. My distorted reflection displayed upon it.

"Some of us remained more fait'ful to de cause," Atholeeon said with pride.

"Perhaps they were still faithful to *a* cause," I retorted. "Their own."

Atholeeon's chest raised with a breath. "Interestin' way to look at it." His eyes found my satchel. "We're still fait'ful to de real cause, Bellwound. We'll guard de Mezar so none of de Fallen Stars can find it. Yer parents left wit' it and buried it away from all of us. Ye don't have to carry dis burden alone."

A sinking feeling shot down my stomach. The idea of leaving the Mezar in this place—with these people—hurt me. I gripped the strap of the satchel and stepped away from him, confused as to why the Mezar had come to mean so much to me in so little time.

"It'll consume ya, little Bellwound," Atholeeon said. "Even rusted and locked, de Mezar will take hold of ye. De longer ye keep it, de more it'll mean to ye. Yer life will be bound to it. Dat's why we had to find ya. It's meant to stay hea'."

"You never thought about seeking out our parents?" Arnon asked. "If you cared so much about them and this Mezar thing, why didn't you pay them a visit in Heedeon?"

Atholeeon's face went rigid. "Do ye doubt de air ye breathe, young Arnon?"

"No," he replied.

"But ye know it's real."

"Yes."

"I'm de air in yer lungs. Ye don't have to see or understand everyt'ing to know t'ings are real." I didn't miss Atholeeon's trembling hand slowly curling into a fist. "And no matter what ye think," he continued. "De truf's dat jus' like stories change us, de Mezar will slowly take over Bellwound. His very breaf keeps it alive, but his life can also destroy it."

"What's on the other side?" Arnon twisted the knob, clearly hoping to stray away from the subject.

"De rooms are empty. We cleaned 'em out after dey left."

"You simply threw everything away?" I asked.

"Dey t'rew deir purpose away, little Bellwound," Atholeeon said, his voice as cold as his face. "We kept a close eye on ye because we're good, but we can't change de outcome of a harvest. Dey planted deir seeds."

"But you seem to think it's up to you to decide the fate of any harvest," I said.

"Da'ts de reason why de Fait' chose me to be de head of dis Council," he said. "Me young ones, trust me. Yer safe here. Dere's much ye don't know about de Dove and de Lion and de Mezar."

Arnon walked into one of the rooms. From floor to ceiling to furnishings, everything was white. The windows faced a forest, displaying a bright blue sky.

"Helga's room," Atholeeon said.

Arnon meandered around, gazing as if trying to imagine his mother wandering this place. He ran a hand over the railings of the bed, the mantel of the fireplace, and the wardrobe tucked in the corner.

"They left because they wanted to?" Arnon asked.

"Dey made deir decision de moment they fell in love and *acted* on it," Atholeeon replied with a smug smile.

There was a strange mixture of sorrow and arrogance when Atholeeon spoke of our parents. He missed them. I could tell that much, but he also seemed proud of the judgement that came upon them—as if something of the sort would never happen to him.

"Where will we be staying?" I asked, hoping he would stop showing us around.

"Oh, ready to retire, are ye?" Atholeeon asked.

"We're exhausted," I said. "And if there's going to be a feast, then we'd rather be rested."

Atholeeon led us back to the hall with all the satin curtains and marble statues. At its very end was a door leading to a hall like the one we had just been in. He opened the first door to our right. "One of you can stay in dis room," Atholeeon waved his hand inside. "And de other one in de room in front of it. We always keep dese rooms ready for guests."

"Get many visitors here?" I asked snidely as Arnon and I stepped into the first room.

"De ones dat matter. Fresh clot'es are inside the clot'es keeper." I assumed he meant wardrobe but didn't bother asking. "Help yerselves to whatever ye prefer. If we don't see each ot'er, dinner will be at seven. I'll send someone to fetch ye."

"Thank you," I said.

"Feat'ered blessin's to ye." He shut the door.

"What a strange man," Arnon said.

I strolled around. The black wallpaper was covered in velvet swirls. Candles burned in the ironclad lamps clinging to the wall.

"Strange he knew we were coming, no? But couldn't see our parents going." Arnon said.

"What happened to being at ease?" I gazed at the mountain ranges outside the window. "There's a lot we don't know, an entire world we've never seen, and our lives are bound to its secrets. I fear there are many."

"You trust them with the Mezar?" Arnon asked.

"No. It makes me sad when I think about parting from it."

"What do you mean?"

"Like I'd be leaving a pet behind," I said. "One I have cared for my whole life. I need to know it will be safe."

"You've never liked pets."

"Leave it up to you to remember everything." I sat on the edge of the bed.

"We've been around each other our whole lives." He sat beside me. "I remember lots." He placed an arm over my shoulders. "Strangely, the Mezar has been with you your whole life. You just didn't know it was there."

I followed his dark braid down to his shoulders. Stubs of hair grew on the shaved sides of his head. He had a hint of a beard. He tugged me closer, the warmth of his breath brushing my face.

I'd never pushed the boundaries of our friendship. Never tried for a kiss. Never tried holding his hand. I had seen him with girls before, and he had seen me with boys. But we had never been with each other. I always feared that pushing those boundaries would open a rift between us.

On the other hand, he would always throw an arm around me whenever I was worried or upset. It was his way of telling me all would be well in the end. He ran a finger over the scar on my left brow, another habit of his. I assumed that, in his mind, it was his way of always apologizing for pushing me into that lake.

I tried to refrain from smiling, but I failed miserably.

"What?" He chuckled.

"Just remembering things," I said.

He smiled wider, flashing me those dimples. "Good things?"

My memories were replaced with desire. It was no longer about holding back a smile. It was about holding an arm over my crotch and willing myself to stay soft beside him.

"You know what I wish?" I started, hoping to distract myself. "I wish I could know when things would end. I wish I would've known that dinner on my Blood-date would be the last time we would all gather. I wish that night at the pub where you kissed Tonelly and I ended up with—"

"With Bart. Of all the boys in Heedeon," he said behind a laugh.

"I wish I'd known that was the last time we'd be doing those things."

His grip on my shoulder tightened. "Why do you say that?"

"So..." I shuddered. "I could've enjoyed them more."

"But not knowing when things end gives us a chance to take risks."

"But then you risk losing something you're not willing to lose."

"I'll say this," he said. "I'm glad to not be discovering all these secrets alone."

"It is good to have you here," I agreed.

"I'm going to take a bath and freshen up," he said, standing.

"See you soon."

"See you."

I remained rooted to the spot after he left, looking up at the ceiling of the room that had once served as a canvas. Above me was an image created to spark dreams of desire—naked men and women gathered in a forest, their only attire the masks on their faces. They were all so unique. Some had horns, others had long noses, and a few had no eyes or lips. Their hands were on each other's breasts, buttocks, and cocks, with fingers buried deep between the legs of the women. In the middle were two naked men wrapped in a longing embrace.

I tossed my satchel on the floor and fell back on the bed. I pulled up my shirt as there was a throb between my legs. My fingertips trailed over my stomach, making their way past my belly button, following the soft trail of hair that disappeared beneath my pants.

I was hard with want for Arnon. Being in an unknown place, not knowing what the future held, made me reckless. I was losing my desire and strength to keep my feelings for him at bay.

My hand stroked steadily while my eyes remained fixed on the two men. I had thought of Arnon that way when I was around fourteen. But the first time I saw him with a girl in Heedeon, I let go of any hope.

I wanted to pretend right now. With every stroke and pull, I imagined the two of us kissing, our chests touching, bodies sweating, cocks grinding. I had seen him naked before, so I could picture it all so vividly. The round birthmark on his shaft was hard to forget and—right now—to resist. I remembered the smell of his skin after a hunt, the way his smile carved deep dimples on his cheeks.

I took off my pants, the jerking and tugging becoming more determined. I tightened my grip, imagining the warm feeling of being balls-deep inside him. Imagined being stretched and filled with him inside me. Would he mind if I were to wrap my mouth around his shaft? Would he use my braid to guide my movements or would he let me take the lead? Would his kiss set my heart racing? Or would it stop it completely? How salty would the sweat taste off his skin? What would he whisper to me in bed?

My body tensed. My chin trembled. My cock pulsed, shooting my pleasure onto my stomach.

We all had secrets. This one I'd keep with me for as long as I could, masked like the witnesses on the painting above me.

ORIAH

CHAPTER SEVEN

The study room was empty. She always claimed that's where she would go to not be disturbed by the other Council members. They tended to hover around us. Announcing she was going to study Valleynerian law always gave us room to breathe. Sometimes we kept to our word and studied. Other times, we locked the doors and enjoyed each other's company in ways no one else could.

I walked through halls and around statues, making my way outside. The woods were my destination. But not the edge of the forest where the high towers of the castle were still visible through the canopy. I had to wander deeper, where ferns hid the ground and the trees were so close, they formed a barrier around us.

The gold of her hair mirrored the autumn leaves still clinging to the trees. Her dress was scarlet, like the petals of a rose. Over her shoulders were white pelts with hints of gray in them. She sat on the edge of the old water fountain marred with cracks and mildew. At its center, standing on a platform, was a child with six wings.

Many claimed the child was Lucifer. Others thought it to be Hanell the Creator. I just thought of how disturbing the child's face was—filled with angst and pain.

"I knew you would find me," she said. "We haven't parted from each other like this for ages."

"I remember the first time we stumbled upon this place." I approached her, placing a hand on her back. "We had managed to venture into Valleyner, and yet all you could think of was the expression on the child's face."

"Perhaps it reminded me of what we went through when our parents were killed." She wrapped her hand around my own. "You've seen the boys?"

"Bellwound is very hard-headed and opinionated. He questions everything. The other, Arnon, can be quite reckless. Both are oblivious to the truth, Loghleen. But I must believe we're doing the right thing. We're keeping our word, our promise to Stenan, Seaahra, Pyeus, and Helga."

"And Arnon?" She stood, her gaze meeting mine. "Are the rumors about him true?"

"I am not sure," I replied. "Crocell met us on the way here with a Shadow army." Her eyes widened. "He hinted at the seed of darkness. He wasn't clear about its true meaning, but the boys aren't foolish. They're beginning to question."

"You saw the dead?" she asked.

"Yes."

She stepped away, walking around the water fountain, gaze fixed on the statue of the child. "She's bound to come looking for us." She folded her arms over her chest. "She'll want all of our kind gathered for Lucifer's return. The Nephilins in the north and the ones in the south."

"Do you regret it?" I asked, walking closer. "Leaving the others? Leaving behind what we were meant to live for?"

"Do you?" She fought away the angst on her face. "Now that the time has come?"

"No." I cupped her face between my hands. "I'd never regret any decision made with you, my love. We've seen much darkness in the last two thousand years. Perhaps we'll see the light when all of this is over."

"But do we belong in the light?" She ran a hand down my cheek.

"I'd like to think we can make it our home if we choose. We've been in Heelyan for eighteen years. We've made this place our home, haven't we? I'd like to believe that if we keep the Dove away, then our kind can live even amongst mortals."

There was tenderness in her eyes. "We may not live to see those days, my life." She kissed me. "Those who believe the stories of the diamond-eyed enemies will wage war against us."

"But at least we get to be alive now." My lips brushed hers. "Right now."

Her tongue searched for mine, sliding between my lips. I, without hesitation, let her find it. My hand gripped the nape of her neck while hers slid down my back.

"I remember," I whispered in her ear, "the first time we kissed."

"That's all you remember?" she chuckled, moving her hand from my back to my bulge. "I remember the first time I made this mine." She gripped me with determination.

"I think it's time you make it yours again." I untied the laces of my pants and pulled them down. "It's been days."

Our lips found each other's again as I gently led her to the forest floor. I pulled up her dress, finding she wore nothing underneath.

"Do you always walk around like this, ma'am?" I asked.

"I have since you left, ready for the moment you would return."

Her answer earned another kiss. Then my lips found her legs. I wanted a taste of the nectar between them. My fingers missed her moist silo, and my cock craved hitting her inner limits. She pulled on my hair, forcing me to look up at her while my mouth continued its journey across her thighs.

"My garden needs tending." She smirked.

I burrowed my face between her legs, my nose grazing her lower lips. My tongue crawled inside. My heart rushed. I throbbed. She moaned.

Time was forgotten by us both. Eternity would be well spent here. She pulled on my hair again, her way of telling me to look up at her. She slid her body down so her chest could find mine. She was low enough for me to make my way inside. I obliged. All these years later and being with her still felt like our first time—raw, wild, and passionate.

The autumn chill wasn't enough to keep our sweat at bay. My tongue trailed down her neck, tasting every drop while I remained inside her. She was mine. I was hers. And in that isolated place, concealed from Council eyes and epistle-keepers, we surrendered to each other three more times before returning to the castle.

BELLWOUND

CHAPTER EIGHT

I untwisted the wet braid on my head with trembling hands. Being inside a tub again conjured ghosts I never thought would haunt me. Trivial things like the sight of dawn crawling across the sky and the memory of Ma braiding my hair sent shivers down my body despite the warm water. My last bath had paved the way to disaster. My body behaved as if the same would happen after this one.

I submerged my head after my hair was free. The light leaking through the window became distorted, dancing on the ripples of the water's surface. That's what my life had become—a distorted reflection of a past never revealed to me.

Once I came up for air, my eyes spotted the satchel and pants I'd tossed on the floor. I was tempted to think of Arnon one more time, but the image of the Mezar filled my head.

Thinking about the symbol of the crown with its two wings and the patterns etched on its rusty surface calmed my nerves. My heart slowed and the trembling stopped. I imagined my parents fleeing this place, crossing the forest and the borderline while holding on to the Mezar. Yes, it belonged to Lucifer, but what led them to flee so far if he wasn't here?

The Mezar. Having it near brought peace like a child being lulled to sleep by a soft lullaby. I felt as if I could plunge into the darkest abyss or swim in the deepest waters, and I would have enough strength to withstand it all. In the peace, I saw a flame hovering over the bed. Another joined. I remained unbothered as fire and smoke spread, leaving me untouched. My senses told me to run, but I remained still, watching the inferno.

The flames died down, revealing a ground of ash and dust. There were no trees, no wind, no sky. I was naked, though no longer in the tub. My feet were buried beneath the ash. But in front of me, among the gray and black, were wings that quivered while the bodies they clung to shared a passionate kiss. They were naked, unbothered by the cinders.

The one with lighter skin and darker hair was on the bottom, his body covered in skin stories that resembled roots and lightning. I remembered the stories about the warriors of old. Only those of high prestige had skin stories on their flesh. Every line, swirl, and figure were meant to symbolize a tale.

His fingers curled, digging into the ash. The one on top of him also had markings on his body, but his were the same gold shade as his hair and glistened with his every move. They both grunted as the golden one gently moved back and forth. He grabbed the other man's shoulders and pushed forward to whisper something in his ear.

That's when their bodies burst into particles of light that merged in the air. The dark-haired one turned into a flying dove. The other was a lion that chased the bird as it ascended. The animal's roar forced me back into the water.

I was in the tub. The satchel was still on the floor, but next to my pants were the Mezar and my dagger. Maybe they had been there the entire time. I had been so consumed with my lingering thoughts that perhaps I hadn't noticed them.

"A dream." I whispered to myself. The hot water of the bath had most likely lulled me into a brief sleep.

It was time to stop the wondering. I got out of the tub, dried myself, and searched for something to wear to dinner. The wardrobe—or the clothes keeper as Atholeeon called it—had a broad selection, some too long to fit me.

I picked one of the nice white shirts. I had never touched such smooth fabric. Then there was a dark brown coat that draped to my knees. On its sleeves, sewn in gold, were vines that converged into wings on the back. I picked black pants that were a little loose and boots that were one size too big.

A knock on the door startled me while I laced my pants. Arnon was on the other side, dressed and ready. He had picked a brown suede jerkin and pants and boots like mine.

"The braid is gone," he said, surprised.

"It was looking too ruffled," I said. "But yours looks… fresh."

"You know a lot of my secrets, but I never told you that my mother taught me to braid." He walked inside and closed the door behind him while I returned to the clothes keeper. "Nothing as fancy as your Blood-date's, but still nice enough for tonight."

I stared at myself in the mirror. "This castle seems too nice for me to have dinner with what was starting to look like a crow's nest on my head."

"Planning on wearing your hair down then?" Arnon asked.

"Not anymore," I said. "Now that I know of your braiding skills."

A smile took his lips. He approached, standing behind me. Our eyes locked in the mirror. I shuddered as his fingers combed through my damp hair. We enjoyed the quiet as he carefully separated my hair into three. He didn't dare pierce the silence even while twisting the braid. Our eyes would meet, and when they did, a smirk found our lips. Arnon was fully clothed but, in my head, he was naked. Never had I thought of him that way so often.

The braid was done, but he stayed in place, resting a hand on my shoulder instead. I didn't know if he expected me to step away, but I didn't want to move. I liked having him behind me. He sucked air through his teeth as if trying to get something off of his chest. "You look good." He turned me around. "Better than before. You might need a shave." I thought he was talking about my chin until he ran a hand across the side of my head. "Your hair grows fast."

"If only the hair on my face did the same."

He laughed and sat on the edge of the bed. Arnon was hairier than I was. He had a full beard at sixteen. My naked face had become the subject of mockery and jokes when it decided to remain a baren wasteland after his had turned into a forest.

He picked up the Mezar and my dagger from the floor. My body tensed as he scanned the etchings on its rusty cover, his thumb following the outline of the winged crown. I sat at his side, confused as to why I felt as if he was about to steal the Mezar from me.

The sun set outside the window, hiding behind the mountain ranges. Amidst the reddish hue were hints of gold and brown. Arnon's gray eyes cooled and contrasted the sunset like the brightening moon. They were locked with mine.

A knock on the door.

"Time for dinner," Arnon said, disappointment in his voice.

"Sad we're going to eat?" I walked to the door.

He nodded, seemingly upset with my question.

A woman was on the other side. Her clear ocean eyes were like sharp blades. Her golden hair was gathered in a mound on top of her head, braided in the back, and fell over her shoulder like a waterfall. Pink cheeks and cherry lips forced me to stare for longer than I would've liked.

"Atholeeon wanted me to fetch you both for dinner," she said.

"Lead the way," I replied, glancing at the small red rose perched in the thin tiara on her head. A red pelt coat dropped to her knees, revealing a blouse embellished with jewels and heeled boots.

Arnon joined me at my side. If I had some yarn, I would've tied his chin up with a bow atop his head to keep his jaw attached.

"I'm Loghleen," the woman said, clearly uncomfortable with Arnon's admiration.

"Right." Arnon mumbled.

I nudged him in the ribs with an elbow.

"Sorry." He cleared his throat. "Arnon."

"Bellwound."

"I was asked to warn you that masks will be given out at dinner," she said. "Tonight is when the Council celebrates the Fiery Glory. I assume you know what that is."

"A celebration of Lucifer's banning from Valleyner," Arnon said. "Right?"

"Correct," she said. "Blessed be the Lion."

"Blessed be the Lion," Arnon mumbled.

"….be the Lion," I repeated a second too late.

I had no memory of ever learning about the Fiery Glory. By the dragon, I should've spent more time reading the books written by the Faith.

We followed her down the hall. The clicking of her boots on the floor was the only sound exchanged between us.

She led us to double doors with golden knobs shaped like a lion's head. But it was the two creatures beside the doors that caused my body to tense. They were pale, faceless, and hairless, with scrawny naked bodies. Their long arms clung to spears. Masks were tied around their wrists. They slowly stretched out an arm—a sign for us to choose one.

I trembled at my distorted reflection scattered over their skin. I didn't know if they noticed the staring. Arnon wasn't as great at concealing his expressions. His eyes bulged, his jaw so low, a rat could've made his mouth a home.

The creature to my right had three black masks hanging from its wrists. One called my attention more than the others. It was crafted to cover the upper part of the face. Wings extended from its sides—the wing on the left looking more ruffled than the one on the right.

Arnon picked a mask like mine, but instead of wings, there were horns. Loghleen chose the simplest of them all. No patterns or etchings or intricate objects arose from it. It was sleek, black, and crafted to conceal the right side of her face.

Once the three of us had our masks on, the scrawny creature opened the door. There were more of its kind inside, gathered on the left corner of the dining hall holding musical instruments. Two played skin-headed drums. Another had a long stringed instrument that, when played by its skeletal hands, sounded like the low rumble of thunder.

The remaining two sang. They had no facial features or movement, but the raising of their chests and shoulders indicated they were responsible for the ethereal vocals. One voice was deep and ominous, and the other gentle and precise.

Loghleen went left, walking toward Oriah who raised a glass when he saw us. Oriah's mask had two elk horns wrapped in a thin golden chain.

The other seven Council members had cups in hand and were already too drunk to greet us properly. Their robes, capes, and jewels of different shapes and sizes all shared the same shades of red and black.

Atholeeon sat in the middle, still sober. He was the only one in a white mask. It covered half his face and forehead, leaving his left cheek in view. Three wings clung to the left side, curving above his head. He stood, spread out his arms, and shouted, "Welcome, welcome to Fiery Glory, me boys!" He pointed at the two empty chairs on the far right of the table. "Sit, sit, sit. And eat."

"By the dragon," Arnon said. "We're going to be carried to our rooms tonight."

"We just need to pace ourselves," I said. "We can't have strangers putting us to bed."

The chairs were of a reddish-brown wood, their top rails carved in the shape of wings. I dragged one of the chairs out and took a seat. Arnon did the same. The table was laden with platters of meats, vegetables, fruits, desserts, and pastries.

My fork carved into the pork. Arnon stuck his into the chicken. Two of the faceless creatures approached us with a decanter of wine. They filled our cups quickly and retreated out into the hall.

"Pay 'em no mind," Atholeeon said, dangling a hand in the air. "Dey're de Obsynth. All dey do here in 'eelyan is serve. Dey do as dey're told and everyone's happy." He turned and started a conversation with the Council member sitting beside him.

"Alright." Arnon raised his cup in the air. "A toast between us then."

"To staying alive," I said while raising mine.

"Come on, Bellwound. That's what we're toasting to?"

"Have a better idea?" I chuckled.

He smirked. "To taking chances?"

"To taking chances," I said.

If I closed my eyes, I could've fooled myself into thinking I was back in Heedeon, drinking at the pub with him. It had been days since I had heard laughter and music together.

I allowed myself to indulge in the illusion of peace. I drank and ate and drank some more. The room began to spin, but the taste of the wine was hard to resist.

Oriah dragged Loghleen out of her chair and to the center of the room. Perhaps they called their spinning and jumping a dance. They shook and quivered their shoulders from side to side in between steps. The other members of the Council joined. Atholeeon remained in his seat, clapping and drinking, his food untouched.

"I swear to Hanell or any other god out there," Arnon said with a mouth full of chicken, "that if that Atholeeon man doesn't eat his food, I will."

"You have plenty on your plate."

"I may need more." He burped. "I'm starving."

I cackled, taking another sip of my wine. Oriah and Loghleen shared a kiss. The other Council members continued the strange dance, a few of their movements friendly, others more determined. You knew a few wanted each other in bed. The tension was visible in the eyes behind the masks, in the gentle swaying of their hips, in the closeness of their lips as their bodies writhed with one another.

"Fuck this." Arnon beat a fist on the table. "Let's dance."

"Drunk talk," I said. "Time to stop."

"Dragonshit." He grabbed my wrist and pulled me to my feet, his body wobbling. "Come on."

Atholeeon clapped with excitement when we joined the others. "Blessed be de feat'ers dat falls over ye!" He shouted, swinging his cup in the air, spilling wine over the table.

Loghleen and Oriah's lips were still locked. The Council members were too taken by each other to notice Arnon and I joining them. The two men beside us had their hands on each other's hips. Their grinding bulges were no secret. They couldn't sleep with each other, but perhaps touching was allowed.

Arnon grabbed my chin, turning my gaze to his. His eyes looked at me with longing—something I had never seen before. My gaze flitted away. He leaned into my ear and whispered, "You can look at me." His breath smelled like the wine.

A battle raged inside me. The wine could be the culprit behind his words. But maybe it was also the wine that gave him the guts to say what he truly meant. Had I missed the signs? Had I been too involved in my own thoughts that I never noticed what Arnon truly felt for me?

My hands trailed down his back, settling on his waist though I was tempted to go lower. I was a couple inches taller, but when I pulled him close, his bulge pressed perfectly against mine. And he was hard.

My will to resist disappeared. My waist moved forward. He repeated the movement. His hand found the nape of my neck, giving me goosebumps, while a finger stroked my earlobe. The laces on my pants struggled to stay in place, pressed through with desire.

I had gone from avoiding my lust for Arnon to wanting him just as fast. The tip of our noses touched. I took in his breath. He playfully burrowed his fingers behind the waist of my pants one at a time. His hips never stopped moving. We danced with our knees knocking, legs weaving. I wanted him completely. I wanted him bare, naked, skin pressed against mine. I didn't care about our audience.

But desire was replaced with shock. Standing in the corner of the room, leaning against the wall, was a man clothed in gray rags. Over his head was the skull of a horned dragon—the snout long and the horns thin and scraggly like tree roots. Blood trickled from beneath the helmet, snaking down his neck. His sleeves weren't long enough to conceal the cuts and bruises on his dark skin. His gaze was locked on me. No one acknowledged his presence as the music continued. He raised a finger in the air and gently brought it to where his lips would be—a sign I should remain quiet.

I stopped moving, my hand still on Arnon's waist.

"Are you alright?" he asked with the hint of a smile. The man vanished at his words.

My desire for Arnon wasn't enough to pull my eyes back to him. I searched the room. Nothing.

"Bellwound?" Arnon insisted.

"Mind if we sit for a bit? I think the wine is making me see things." My eyes remained where the man had stood.

Arnon followed my gaze over his shoulder. "And by the look on your face, not something very pleasant."

We returned to our seats. A few of the Council members followed while the others continued to dance and laugh. One of the Obsynth attempted to fill my cup, but I refused. The image of the man was too strong in my mind.

Everything set me on edge. The singing, the obnoxious laughter, the masks—even the way the Obsynth played their music. Arnon wanted to talk. He kept giving me fleeting glances, probably wondering what to say. He put a hand over mine and pursed his lips, looking confused. He didn't need to speak for me to know my behavior concerned him.

"Attention!" Atholeeon shouted with a clap. "Attention, all *dancers* in de room."

Laugher erupted.

"We've eaten. We've drank. Now 'tis time to honor de Lion. To remember de day of reckonin' when Valleyner was cleansed of wickedness."

Everyone in the room wobbled their way back to their seats.

"Blessed be Hanell's holy feathers," said one of the Council members, beating a fist on the table before taking a seat. "For they protect us from evil."

"Blessed be," all repeated, some slurring the words.

Arnon's hand stayed on mine as a fire burned in me, an angry flame, untamed and fast spreading. The man I had seen haunted my thoughts. I thought about the Mezar—how it waited for me in the room. I found comfort in knowing I would soon return to it, and unease in thinking the man might return to me. My thoughts must have manifested him. He was back, wandering around the table and observing every person present.

"Do you see him?" I whispered to Arnon.

"Who?"

"The masked man."

"Everyone's in a mask here, Bellwound." He tightened his grip around my hand.

His gesture drew my eyes. I followed the creases on his knuckles, noticing the cracks on his fingers. His thumb gently grazed my skin, the gesture soothing me slightly. I had lost sight of the man but knew he still remained.

An abrupt silence settled before the Obsynth with musical instruments changed the song. The festive tunes were replaced by somber notes accompanied by beating drums.

"Time to cleanse our minds." Atholeeon clapped. The Obsynth returned to the room with decanters in hand, pouring a clear liquid into our cups.

"Drink," Atholeeon ordered. "And be cleansed. Be sober."

The other Council members drank at his command. Oriah and Loghleen waited for them to finish before they obeyed. I drank the bitter beverage, cringing as it stung its way down my throat.

"What's in this? Dragon piss?" My question earned a chuckle from Arnon.

It was as if a river rushed in me, taking with it the brief joy the wine had brought me along with the anger. The smiles faded across the room. Slouching bodies assumed rigid postures and frowns formed on every face.

Four Obsynth entered the room, holding a stretcher made of wicker with warped wooden handles and overflowing with dead white doves. They set it on the floor in front of the dinner table.

"Blessed be dy holy feat'ers of mercy," Atholeeon began. "And dy claws of justice. Mig'ty is the mane dat drapes below dy chin. From its tips drips the dew of truf."

The Council members repeated his words. Oriah and Loghleen remained quiet, watching.

"Cursed is de Dove born from a flower," Atholeeon continued. "For he was the source of evil and discord. Praise be to Hanell de Creator and mig'ty Lion for his was the judgement dat cast de traitor into the fire."

The long arms of the Obsynth who had carried the stretcher abandoned their skeletal shape, taking on the role of sharp blades.

"Dy winged crown reminds us dat de power in blood speaks louder dan de breath in our lungs. Yours is the immortal crown, for yer kingdom will never end. And before ye, all will bow."

They chopped the birds. There was no rhythm to their action. They simply sliced them, sending feathers in the air and spilling blood on the floor.

Atholeeon clapped. The other Council members joined. Oriah did the same, but his claps weren't as determined as the rest. They were slow. His eyes didn't need to be in full view for me to notice his resistance to what took place. Loghleen remained still, arms dangling over the arms of her chair.

The movements of the Obsynth grew faster and fiercer. All reveled in the mutilation of the animals. But of course, it wasn't the slicing of birds that brought them joy. It was the notion that the birds represented Lucifer, and *they* were the ones to bring him to justice.

"And we must celebrate hea' tonight," Atholeeon said over the applause. "De Mezar being brought back to us. After so long, it's been brought to de safest place it could be." He laced his fingers together and swayed his hands as if begging. "Oriah, t'ank ye for bringin' Bellwound and Arnon to safety. Ye know dat der parents were dear to us hea'."

Oriah tapped two fingers on his forehead before bringing his hand down to rest on his chest—a sign that Atholeeon was more than welcome for his deed.

"You're leaving the Mezar here?" Arnon whispered.

"I don't remember that being discussed."

"And in order to honor ye both," Atholeeon continued. "We've had de Obsynth bring to ye a rare delicacy. 'Tis not of Valleynerian origin, but of our mortal world, Thestlen. The Lion's Fang is the purest wine ye'll ever taste. Back in Metra, it was said dat de blood of de Creator himself was used to make such a drink."

An Obsynth set two golden grails next to us. The others were served as well, but their grails were silver.

Loghleen stared from across the table. She didn't blink. She didn't move. She was shrouded in curiosity and confusion, her attention on the grail in front of me.

97

"Now, a toast. To Bellwound and Arnon!" Atholeeon lifted his cup, the others following suit. "May de blessin's of old be with ye—"

"Before we all drink." Loghleen got up from her seat. "Why don't you taste it first, Atholeeon?"

Atholeeon was confused.

"As a good host, which I know you are," she said. "I thought it would be wise to drink the wine before any of us do. If memory serves me right, The Lion's Fang, if not fermented properly, can easily turn into poison."

All gazed at her, bewildered.

"Are ye implyin' what I think ye are, my dear?" Atholeeon set his cup on the table and removed his mask.

"A mere suggestion." She shrugged, revealing her face as well. "I've been alive for many years, as you know. In not one of them do I remember a hint of silver bubbles in The Lion's Fang. It's supposed to be as scarlet as blood. Do correct me if I'm wrong."

The corners of Atholeeon's lips trembled. He bit down on his upper lip, rage filling his eyes. "I was de one chosen to man dis Council durin' dis time." The veins in his neck were visible under his skin. "I was brought hea' from Metra to serve. Ye don't get to tell me what to do in me own home."

The Council members muttered amongst each other. One by one, they set their masks on the table.

"Drink it," I said, my own mask now discarded.

Atholeeon's eyes widened. "I beg yer pardon?"

"After all we've been through," I said. "I'm sure you don't think much of the request, right?"

"I'm sure yer parents taug't ye not to tell a host w'at to do."

"My parents taught me much. Both etiquette and survival."

"To be told what to do in me own home—"

"Your home?" Loghleen scoffed. "You see, I've seen many men and women rise and fall, live and die. You're but a small breath in all the long years I've lived. Your home? More like your temporary shelter. And what about the other members of the Council sitting at this table? Is this not their home as well? Do they, too, agree that you should drink from the wine first?"

Silence.

Atholeeon walked away from his seat and came my way. He picked up the grail in front of me and went to her, the silence still looming.

"Ye t'ink ye know all dere's to know about me," Atholeeon said. "Ye with yer long years in this world. But ye don't know everythin'. I know w'at is better now. I know w'at needs to be done. De time has come for me to stand in de truth."

He spilled the wine from my cup onto her face. At first, I thought it the impulsive response of someone very privileged. But the wounds that started appearing on her face said otherwise. She screamed as her skin turned to steam, rising into the air as little wisps.

Two Obsynth rushed to Oriah's side. His breath was driven out of his body as the creatures stabbed his shoulders with their steel hands. The other Council members didn't get a chance to protest.

The Obsynth plunged their steel hands into their hearts as they realized that tonight was to be their last. Regret and longing reflected from their pupils as they faced each other while dying.

Atholeeon revealed two chains from under his robe and whipped them over Loghleen's wrists. Her skin sizzled beneath them as she fell to her knees.

I rose to my feet, regretting having left my dagger in the room.

"Ye move and she's dead," Atholeeon said.

"Fucking traitor!" Arnon shouted.

"Stupid fuckin' kids," Atholeeon said, eyes on Loghleen. "Nephilins are beautiful," he taunted. "But ye and Oriah are de black sheep of yer kind. Ye bring dem so much disappointment. Ye could've tortured dose two 'til dey agreed to do what dey were always meant to do." He slapped her face, before beckoning an Obsynth closer with the curl of a finger. "Take de cunt below. De Nephilin queen will be happy to deal with her later."

Its bony fingers grabbed Loghleen by the hair and dragged her out. Her arms quivered. Wounds had formed around the chains on her wrists.

Oriah's screams had turned to shudders. He fell from his seat, landing on his left shoulder. The two Obsynth kept their blade hands lodged in him. I could see him from under the table, hands shaking, a puddle of blood widening around him.

We were next.

"Pity," Atholeeon said. "I didn't plan for t'ings to happen like dis. Ye, little Bellwound, who bears sacred blood. And ye, Arnon, privileged to be a vessel for darkness. I trust de Dove, ye see? I trust de Lion, too. But I also trust me. All I got to do was to remain cooped up in dis forsaken castle. But now, wit' de Mezar, its bearer, and de seed of darkness under my roof, I'll get to tell the gods w'at to do."

"You're insane," I said.

"It's insanity dat gives men courage, little Bellwound." He chuckled. "Is de Mezar in your room?"

The very thought of Atholeeon holding the Mezar replaced my fear and confusion with rage. It had been in my house for almost two decades. It belonged to *me*. By the dragon, the idea of parting from the cursed object weighed me down. Oddly, parting with it would feel like losing one of my own limbs.

Roars echoed outside the walls of the castle. Atholeeon listened to the emerging sound, fear filling his face.

The stained-glass windows exploded, scattering shards across the dining hall. Fire and smoke hid the ceiling. The roars continued as the inferno raged. A winged creature flew into the room, its wings wide and mighty. I could see them through the smoke, covered in feathers of gray and brown. Its face and mane belonged to a lion, its golden eyes glimmering like a flame in the dark. A breomer. I had read about them. Not in the books of Faith, but in stories of adventure. It was an animal believed to only exist in the pages of old.

It landed atop the dining table, breaking it in half. Its mighty roar sent the Obsynth away. The scrawny creatures didn't dare protest. They released us from their hold and fled the room, leaving Atholeeon to fend for himself.

Arnon and I ran to Oriah's aid. Strength returned to him once he was freed from the blades. His skin regained its hue, his lips their color.

"I serv'd dis place well!" Atholeeon shouted. "In all my years of servitude, I begged to see a breomer." The veins in his neck swelled. "And ye dare send one to kill me!" he shouted. "Fuck you, Hanell. And you, Lucifer. Fuck ye all."

Flames erupted from the animal's mouth, wrapping him in a fiery cocoon. His screams echoed for a few seconds, replaced by the crackling of his robes and body.

"Are you alright?" I helped Oriah stand while four more breomer flew into the room, casting flames on the curtains and chairs. They were angry, burning everything in sight. They had come not for prey, but for vengeance.

"The hall!" Oriah shouted. "The hall!"

We fled left, darting across the room before the flames grew too powerful. We ran down the hall. Oriah struggled to keep our human pace, wanting to remain true to his speed. He ran ahead and slowed down once he realized we were too far behind him.

The smell of smoke and burnt flesh lingered. Their roars echoed, daring my heart to beat faster.

"Where'd those things come from?" Arnon asked behind heavy breaths once we were far from the fire.

"I don't know," Oriah answered.

"The Mezar is in my room," I said. "I need to get it."

"Then let's go get it," Oriah said. "We have someone else to rescue."

We raced pasts columns, statues, and paintings, coming to the hall with all the rooms. I swung the door open, relieved that the satchel and dagger were on my bed.

I ran inside with Arnon. I flung the flap open. The Mezar was inside. I tossed it over my shoulder, my urge to escape suddenly replaced by fear. He was back—the man with the dragon skull. He stood in the corner, as still as the statues in these halls. Blood dripped down his neck, creating a puddle on the floor.

"By the dragon." Arnon's eyes widened.

I grabbed Arnon's wrist and pulled him with me as I headed out.

We ran down the opposite side of the hall, Oriah leading us away from the sound of the breomer's roars.

The sight of a white marble statue depicting a kneeling winged warrior brought us to a halt. It had one hand outstretched, the other clinging to a spear.

"Fire, doom, desire," Oriah said, touching the empty hand. "Take us deeper. Take us higher. Spare us from the curse of the deep. Light our pace. Guide our feet."

The statue dispersed in the air like snow, its flakes spinning around us. Everything in sight was replaced by a thick darkness.

CHAPTER NINE

A small golden glare glistened in the shadows, growing wider until the word *Peritas* appeared on the rusty surface of an iron door. The word had been carved, but every letter was comprised of many lines, as if whoever carved them struggled to do so. Beneath the word were bones, randomly scattered, forming the shape of a lion's head.

"Peritas," I mumbled.

"It means justice in the ancient Valleynerian tongue of Ozrah," Oriah said.

The door creaked open on its own, a putrid odor seeping through its widening crevice. Flames burned bright on torches clinging to pillars, revealing a long hall made of stone with a river flowing in the middle.

Oriah cautiously stepped ahead, Arnon following after him. The entire structure of the prison trembled once Arnon was past the doorway.

"What was that?" he asked as I joined him.

"The prison senses danger," Oriah said.

"What, I'm dangerous?" Arnon shot me a worried glance.

"Aren't we all?" I said.

We followed the rushing water. If I closed my eyes, the trickling sound of the river could've fooled me into believing I was back in Heedeon, sitting by the river, fishing with Da, but the foul smell kept me present.

Voices whispered, groaned, quivered. To the left of me were barred cells. Inside each one was the bronze statue of a six-winged lion with wide bowls beneath them.

"Don't mind them," Oriah said. "They're echoes of those who perished in this horrid place."

"Not sure if that makes things better or worse," I said.

"And the lion statues?" Arnon asked. "What are those for?"

"Torture," Oriah said. "Those bowls are filled with coal and set aflame. There's a small door on the rear of each statue. Criminals would be placed inside and roasted to death. They crafted the statues so the tortured screams of the imprisoned, when burned, sounded like lion roars."

The structure of the prison trembled again, spilling the water of the river into a few of the cells around us. The cells stretched far ahead. They were also across the river running deeper into the prison. I pressed my hand against the Mezar in my satchel as if it could rescue me from this place. Even through the leather, I could feel its rusty edges.

The sounds of the dead grew louder in my ears. My grasp tightened around the Mezar. Whispers turned into screams. I wanted them to stop, but I also wanted them to continue. I wanted to see the truth of Oriah's story about this place. I never expected my wish to be granted.

Suddenly, I was inside one of the cells. I was a spectator. The Obsynth and the naked woman were the main act. The creature guided her to the back of the bronze six-winged lion, holding one of its blade hands against her back. Her face was red and puffed, eyes still wet. She walked to stand in front of the hinged door on the rear of the statue. Her hands trembled as she crawled inside. The Obsynth closed the door and knelt on the floor, placing the tip of its blade hands inside the bowl. He struck them against each other, as if they needed to be sharpened, but the movement caused sparks that lit the coal.

"Bellwound!" Arnon's voice beckoned me out of the vision. His hand was around my wrist, his face full of worry and confusion. "By the dragon, are you alright?"

I took in a ragged breath and quickly surveyed the prison. No Obsynth. No woman. Just the three of us and the voices.

"Yes," I said. "I was just thinking."

Oriah frowned, noticing my grip around the Mezar. "Are you afraid it's going to run away?"

A cloud of gray smoke crawled out of the river, permeating the prison quicker than wildfire. It moved as if it had limbs of its own. It latched around the bars of each prison cell, dissolving them like melting ice. As iron turned to liquid, so did the lion statues. A sentient darkness followed into each cell, acting as a shroud that suddenly lifted to reveal bodies piled on top of each other. The hovering smoke disappeared once the dead were all in view.

The scattered torches cast shadows over the bodies. Blood, bruises, and gashes marred each one. From children to elders, they were strewn about like waste. The putrid stench brought water to my eyes. Arnon gagged, holding a fist over his mouth.

"Atholeeon was a traitor this entire time," Oriah said in anger. "He helped them build a Shadow army in Heelyan."

I didn't want to keep staring at the dead, but curiosity held me captive. I didn't want to look at their mutilated bodies, but I couldn't seem to help myself. I had never seen a dead person before. And now there was a whole army of them.

The pile to my left was mostly made up of women and children. They were all naked, some with blood still dripping from wounds that had never congealed. Out of all of them, the body of one woman in particular drew my attention. Her eyes were still open, green and wide. Her gray hair was stained a wet brownish red and her arm stretched across the floor.

The smoke returned, crawling over the bodies before me. I chanced a look over my shoulder. The smoke whirled in circles, collecting into a human shape: the man with the dragon skull. Oriah was stunned, but found peace when Loghleen appeared beside the man. They ran to each other, kissing and hugging as if they had been apart for ages.

"You're alright." Oriah took her hands and brought her wrists to his eyes. "The wounds healed."

"Yours too," she said with a trembling smile. "I was so worried." She turned toward the dragon skull man. "Thank you, Ely, for getting me out of that bronze lion."

"It was the least I could do." His voice had the same cadence as the echoes of the dead. "Now that I must linger with the dead."

"Ely?" Oriah mumbled. "Ely, where have you been? I went to Heedeon because they said you came back and reported your sighting of Crocell."

"You know him then?" I asked.

"You forget I've always been expendable." Ely let out a ghostly shriek. "Atholeeon killed me when I returned. He needed a puppet to confirm his suspicions. I was a mere spy for the Council after all. But not only did he take my life. He cursed me to live in this forsaken place. And I had to watch him and his twisted ways with the innocent every day in return."

The lower part of Ely's body was like a thin veil, revealing the river on the other side. His face was hidden behind the skull, but even through the narrow gaps of his mask, his eyes reflected the sorrow of his truth.

"Why was I the only one able to see you before?" I asked. "And if you're bound to live in this place, how were you in the dining hall?"

"I was able to leave," he replied. "I suspect it's your presence with the Mezar. I had enough strength to wander, to see what allowed me some freedom. Then I saw you in the dining hall, and I had never felt stronger. And because of you, I'm able to stand here, Bellwound Epistle-Keeper—even in death." He removed his mask, revealing round eyes, full lips, and a gash across his skull that tempted my eyes away from his gaze. "I'd kneel if I could, Lord Bellwound."

"Lord?" I scoffed. "I think you have me mistaken."

"No, I don't. There's a time for all things. A time of innocence, a time to know the truth, a time to avenge the truth, and a time to die for it." His gaze shifted to Arnon. "And without you, Arnon, Bellwound can never be. But the seed in you is growing, and it'll soon pierce the soil. You'll have to cut down the tree before you can burn it. Remember who you are when you cross over to the other side." He winced as if stabbed by a blade.

"What's the matter?" Oriah asked.

"Death is coming." He let out a sharp breath. "It's always on top of me. That ugly, scrawny creature." His eyes darted around the prison. "Fine, fine, fine! I'll leave, damn you."

His body cracked like ice. The dragon skull mask shattered. Deep darkness concealed everything in sight. Our shuddering breaths were the only sound until a raspy breath echoed in the shadows. Something slithered around us. Its warm breath touched my face, raising the hair on my arms. I closed my eyes—a foolish act since I was already lost in the unseen.

Fingers laced with mine. Arnon's. I squeezed his hand and said, "I'm here."

"Visitors? Do we have visitors?" a shrill voice said. "Where d'you come from, eh? Why have you come to see Death?"

None of us replied.

"Oh, I do see now. Visitors don't answer Death. Why d'you fear desperation, eh? I can be your closes' friend. Do not judge I 'cause you can't see I, eh."

Flames appeared above me, hovering like birds. The sound of ragged breaths filled my ears. I followed the eerie sound, my gaze landing on a disfigured being with shriveled skin, golden eyes, and teeth like jewels under the sun. Its arms and hands were too long for its size. And where its legs should be, was the tail of a snake, covered in thin gray stripes.

"My, my, who do we have here, eh?" it whispered. "Bellwound, son of Seaahra and Stenan T'rovar." Its golden eyes watched me and then shifted toward Oriah and Loghleen. "My, my, and hea'? Immortals have come to meet Death?"

"Not by choice." Loghleen observed the creature as it slithered around us in circles.

"What have you done with Ely?" Oriah asked.

"Dat stubborn man." Death hissed. "I not chose to have him hea'. Atholeeon wanted him around. I know not. But when he does not obey, I have me way wit' him."

Arnon tightened his grip on my hand.

"Amusing t'ing—the heart, eh?" Death continued. "It has a will of its own. It can fool ye or inspire ye or kill ye…" Its speech faded into silence once its eyes found Arnon. "Arnon Helvug… this one…

dead… eh?" It smiled. "This one is nigh to crossin' the bridge."

I thought Arnon was going to break my hand.

"Why have *you* come to us?" Loghleen asked.

"Death comes to show ye de door. Not time for ye four yet." The flames dancing above us darted right, forming the shape of a doorway. "Secret ways behin' it. The door will lead ye out, but before it does, ye must see t'ings. You want to see dem?"

"What things?" I asked.

"Secrets," Death whispered.

> *"Oh eyes, for those who don't see*
> *Poor, little, witty hearts that cling to ye.*
> *Through the darkness they shall go*
> *Let darkness take them whole."*

The words carried a strange melody, neither in nor out of tune. My body was pulled into the doorway. I was no longer in the prison. A different nightmare had found me.

Countless bodies were resting on a dry wasteland. There were men, women, and children forming a straight line as far as the eye could see.

"Ye must sees, eh? Ye must sees where dey are," Death whispered. "Spirits lie in t'is dark place. Ye can't leave wit'out knowin'."

The others were nowhere to be seen.

"Only ye get to see t'is. T'ey now see what I want them to. T'ese people lie in cold places while spirits sleep, Bellwound. T'eir bodies will wake mad wit' hunger and vengeance. Ye needed to see. T'eir bodies are in t'e prison, but t'is is where t'eir souls sleep, kept here so t'eir bodies can become Shadows."

"Who's doing this?" I asked in a trembling voice.

Death slowly bowed its head. "Many." It laid a hand on my shoulder.

When I was a child, I fell into a river. I remember being tossed about by the current while struggling to swim to the surface. The water didn't care that I craved air. It bent my will to its own. Death's touch felt the same way. I was jerked out of the nightmare and though I fought to keep control while being pulled upward, my will was disregarded. My stomach was tossed about like an autumn leaf in the wind. My arms flailed in the dark, my hands trying to find something to hold on to.

Despair spread through me. I was alone, hurling through nothing without any direction. A light appeared, growing wider until swallowing the darkness.

My feet found ground. My hands went to my knees. My dinner shot its way into my mouth. I swallowed it back. I kept my head down, waiting for the world to stop spinning. The feast shot up again. I wasn't strong enough to hold it back that time. I wiped the side of my lips with a sleeve. Oriah and Loghleen were to my left, relieved to find me alive. Arnon was on the other side, spewing all his food and wine.

My senses slowly returned to their right place. The white castle was wreathed in flame. Breomers hovered, acting as if they were meant to keep watch over the area and burn any other living thing trying to escape their inferno.

"You saw the bodies?" I asked.

"The ones in the prison?" Loghleen was confused. "We were with you."

"What did you see when Death took you?" I asked as smoke spread across the sky.

"Nothing," she said. "We saw the doorway and walked through it."

Death hadn't lied. I was the only one who had seen the spirits of the dead.

Arnon wobbled closer, hands on his waist. "I'd hug you all if my stomach wasn't such a mess right now."

"I don't care." I rushed his way and threw my arms around him.

He returned my embrace, burying his face between my neck and shoulder.

"You're alright," he whispered repeatedly. "You're alright."

Oriah and Loghleen held hands while the fire consumed the castle. Their diamond eyes were shrouded in sorrow for it had been their home. They had left their own kind to live behind those walls. Now we had all become the same—wanderers in a world full of lies and deceit.

Arnon and I held hands as we walked through the trees. Oriah and Loghleen walked ahead and didn't stop once the mist that brought us to Heelyan appeared. There was lightning inside, bright flashes that skipped in all directions. The mist didn't behave that way the first time we tread through it. Shadows of different shapes appeared in the curtain of white, moving at a speed my eyes couldn't follow.

My lungs couldn't draw breath. My knees buckled. Darkness took me.

CHAPTER TEN

I ran through a green forest. The trees were covered in flowers, pink, white, yellow, and blue bursts of color. The sunlight shone through the canopy, making the grass an even brighter green. It smelled like spring, like damp soil that had just realized it was time to say goodbye to the ice of winter.

"Wait, Bellwound!" said a voice I hadn't heard in a long time. I looked over my shoulder. Arnon ran behind me. He was a child again, wearing a red piece of cloth for a belt around his waist. His thick black hair was cut like a bowl, bouncing while he tried to catch up.

"I know you too well!" I shouted, startled at the sound of my own voice—the voice of a child. "You want me to slow down so you can win!"

We jumped over limbs and rocks as the trees rustled in the wind. A herd of horned rabbits crossed our path, leaping alongside us. The creatures had decided we were all in a race, following us as if playing a game.

Arnon caught up with me with a smug smile on his face. He flicked a finger, running at an even faster pace. My heart raced, not because of my speed, but because of him. Everything about him drew me in. The way he got angry when he was left behind and how he insisted that red cloth around his waist made him look braver than he was.

The world slowed down as I watched that scarlet cloth bounce with his movements. Thread shifted into blood, dripping onto the green forest floor. Everything went dark. Arnon looked over his shoulder, smiled, and burst into ash.

My eyes fluttered open, tears streaming down the sides of my face. It had all been a dream, but the sight in front of me made me question if I had fallen into another. I was looking at a ceiling with paintings of dragon riders fighting soldiers on horses. Two six-winged men shared a kiss in the middle of the carnage. They weren't at war like the rest. They were in love, unbothered by the killings happening around them. Instead of breastplates and gauntlets, they wore white robes. The silhouettes of their bodies were in view under their garments.

I searched the unfamiliar room, chestnut walls and candelabras shaped like vines surrounded me. The window on my left revealed a fog so thick, it hid whatever lay beyond. The palms of my hands traveled across the soft gray satin bed sheet as I sat up.

My undergarments were the only piece of clothing on my body. At the foot of the bed was a neatly folded set of clothes: a black waistcoat, a black leather vest, a gray overcoat, and boots.

I stared into the distance, trying to make sense of how I got there. The lingering smell reminded me of the nights we'd burn handron logs in our fireplace. They cast a sweet scent with a hint of pine and pumpkin.

I dressed myself and walked to a door on the right side of the room.

I rattled the knob, trying to open it. "Damn it." Pounding on the door, I called out, "Anyone there? Hello?" But when no one came, I let out a frustrated grunt before striking the door once more with my fist.

I was suddenly struck with the realization that I hadn't seen my satchel. I whirled around, the door no longer of interest to me, as I feverishly searched the entire room. I overturned the sheets, opened drawers, looked under the bed and behind the black satin curtains draped beside the window. Nothing.

The reality that the Mezar wasn't with me caused my breath to falter. Where had it gone? It was mine. I was its keeper. Who stole it? The shapes in the mist, had they taken it?

A rattling sound came from the other side of the door. The hinges creaked as it opened. A woman stood at the entrance with a key in hand. Her blond hair was braided into thin sections and her ivory skin appeared ordinary at first until I noticed her eyes. Diamond blue eyes. She was one of them. A Nephilin.

"Oh, glad to see you're awake," she said. "Apologies on keeping you locked in here. We had to make sure you weren't going to run off before we get acquainted."

"Did you take it?" I asked as I studied her. "Did you fucking take it, you bitch?"

My sudden burst of rage surprised me.

"By the holy Dove, you're as wild as I thought you'd be," she said behind a chuckle.

A symbol was carved on the golden breastplate covering her cleavage, the same one Oriah had on his clothes when he met me in Heedeon: a circle surrounding a square and a triangle with a cross set in the middle.

"Did you take my satchel?"

"Why, I did, yes." She smiled. "We *found* you after all. We found it and claim all that was in it. I'm amazed you alluded us this long. The Mezar and the dagger are ours now."

"Where am I?" I asked, staring at the white feathers rising from the cuffs of her scarlet coat and only then wondering where Arnon might be.

A smirk appeared on her face. "Sandrovar. I have a map if you need one." Her brow arched in impatience. "But my, you love your questions."

"Name?" I requested.

"How rude of me," she said coldly. "Helstrid. How do you like the clothes? I wanted to make sure they were a good fit. Getting you naked didn't take much effort at all. Now keeping my hands off you—that was an entirely different story. Thankfully, I do have a lot of self-control."

I felt violated but knew I couldn't show any weakness, so I remained silent.

"Alright, not really in the mood to chat." She sighed. "Fine. Now *come*. Your so-called friends await."

I walked past her. She locked the door behind me and rushed her pace to walk ahead.

The hall had been built to intimidate those who tread through it. Red veins crawled on the walls, spreading across the ceiling. Crystal chandeliers were surrounded by colorful art of winged men and women. Ahead hung two scarlet banners beside a door. On them was the same symbol Helstrid wore.

She opened the door, leading me into a crowded room. Those gathered had different skin tones and hair colors, but the piercing blue eyes were consistent. They bowed their heads as I followed Helstrid down an aisle, walking toward a wooden platform supporting a throne carved in the shape of a dove. Behind it was a statue of the six-winged man, his face shrouded in sorrow.

"Now," she started as we walked up the steps of the platform. "Promise me you'll cooperate. Lucifer is very fond of you. He may be patient, but I don't share that trait with him."

"Cooperate with what?" I asked.

"With what I say, of course." She smiled.

How could I protest? I was surrounded by strangers who observed me like prey, defenseless and alone. Where was Arnon? Had they done something to him?

A man strode in from a door to my left. He had olive skin and eyes the same color as hers. Fangs clung to his necklace, jittering with his every step. His brown hair was weaved in parts, falling a little below his pierced ears. Relief found me when Oriah, Loghleen, and Arnon emerged from behind him. Arnon's eyes remained locked with mine until they stopped a short distance from the platform.

"The prodigal children have returned to the nest," Helstrid said.

The man leading them chuckled. "I would've killed these two at this point. What a waste of time."

"Be nice, Borger." Helstrid smirked. "Be nice."

Borger rolled his eyes, dismissive of her comment.

"We've remained hidden for all these years," Helstrid said. "Waiting for Lucifer's return. I thought you two would've remembered your lessons. But you scurried off to the Council because you believed in your own cause." She clapped. "Let this be a lesson to all who want to resort to rebellion," she warned, her voice growing louder with every word.

Oriah and Loghleen kept their heads low, eyes on the ground.

Curiosity and longing filled Helstrid's face as she turned her gaze to Arnon, looking at him like he was a rare jewel. She beckoned him closer with a wave. I was on edge, her every trivial action of sudden interest to me.

"What do you want?" Arnon asked.

"To talk." She grimaced. "Please."

He trudged forward, his knees brushing the edge of the platform. All the while, all I could see was the Arnon from my dream—young, naive, and full of life.

"Mind coming up here?" she requested.

"I can hear you fine," he said.

Her long breath helped her contain her impatience. She reached behind the black throne and removed the Mezar from under it. *My stolen Mezar.* She held it in one hand and, with the other, touched the statue of the six-winged man. Bloody tears started snaking down its face. She held the Mezar under the statue's chin, the act causing the streak of tears to flow like a fountain. A puddle of blood formed at the foot of the statue, spreading to my feet as the Mezar was soaked in scarlet.

Borger grabbed Arnon by the nape of his neck. My hands clenched into trembling fists as he dragged him up the steps of the platform. He was going to walk past me. I could land a punch on the fucker's left cheek—delaying him enough for Arnon to run.

I abandoned reason once Borger was in front of me, dragging Arnon like a hunted trophy. My right fist swung in the air, striking Borger's cheek. A sharp pain zapped up my arm. It was like punching a wall of iron. A smug smile formed on his face as he halted. He laughed. He fucking laughed.

Arnon stretched a hand toward me. I held it briefly, until my muscles seized. My knees buckled. I knelt on the ground, cringing as a wave of torture coursed through me.

"I've had it with you," Helstrid said with a strange calm as my muscles ached. "If you aren't going to behave properly, then I'll force you to be still."

Pain made me a puppet to her unseen power. Borger blew me a kiss and continued toward the statue. He tossed Arnon under the torrent of blood. His entire body ran scarlet in a matter of seconds. He tried to find his feet but was trapped under an invisible weight.

"What're you doing?" Arnon begged.

"The seed of darkness needs to break through the ground," Helstrid said, daring to run her hand over his blood-soaked face while holding the Mezar with the other.

I wanted to run. I wanted to scream. I wanted to kill them. Guilt tried to flood me for thinking of murder, until I made peace with the fact that they weren't people. They were horned rabbits to me, and I was their hunter.

"With all your ingenuity and wisdom, Helstrid," Oriah said from amidst the other Nephilins, drawing Helstrid's attention away from Arnon. "I thought you'd have a will of your own. I thought you would be able to see that we were mere pawns in the master plan of the gods."

Helstrid's face was as cold as a winter's chill. "Traitors." Her face flushed. Oriah let out a pain-filled grunt as he coiled into himself, his body shivering. "How dare you say such a thing? No other Nephilin has abandoned their kind but you and the whore you claim to love. I think you have me confused. Have you forgotten I can make you suffer? Have you forgotten the many times I made you cry? Don't forget who you are. I taught you all you know."

Loghleen jumped up and used the wall to propel herself in Helstrid's direction—her swift movements elegant and rageful. Borger leapt upward like a grayfur-cat trying to kill a dove. He pulled her down by her ankles, her back striking the ground.

"You keep her there," Helstrid said with an edge. "I'm tired of distractions."

"You always torture people to get what you want?" Arnon rose to his feet.

"No, dear one," she replied. "I do it so they can see reason."

She tossed the Mezar in my direction. It landed a palm's length away. I was a dog, the Mezar my bone, and my body unwilling to obey my commands.

Arnon fell to his knees yet again, trembling. A pain-filled grunt followed.

My mind ordered my body to stand—to fucking do something, but no matter how much I fought for my own will, Helstrid's power kept me subdued.

Borger stalked closer, standing beside me, impatiently picking at his thumb. Loghleen stood up, defeated, watching in despair. Arnon's trembling and groaning exploded into screams. My heart wanted out of my chest as much as I wanted to break free from my unseen restraints, but no fear, no desire, and no love was a match for her strength.

"He promised you would come back to me," Helstrid whispered. "He promised he would use some of his power to bring you back. And now I'll get to have you by my side again."

Arnon's screams raised until they cracked into silence. His jaw remained wide, and the veins in his neck bulged. He wobbled back and forth, still on his knees. Helstrid grabbed his hair and forced his head back. She held his mouth open for the blood to pour in. Helstrid gently brought his chin to a close once the blood overflowed, like a mother giving medicinal herbs to her babe. He fell on his side, unconscious.

Borger cackled beside me and unsheathed a dagger from his belt. I shuddered. It was the dragonfang dagger Da had given me. He strode toward Arnon, twirling the weapon in his hand. Time seemed to slow as I followed his every step, listening to his bone necklace rattle.

Borger kicked Arnon on his shoulder, rolling him to his back. The blood streaming from the statue poured over his chest. Borger knelt beside him and raised the marble-white dagger—*my* dagger—so his hand was under the scarlet stream.

He thrust down. The sound of a blade piercing flesh was familiar to me. It meant food on the table. It meant a successful Blooddate. But not today. Sorrow and despair choked me. It took a dagger to his heart for me to acknowledge the love I'd always felt for him. Not friendship, not just complicated desire. Love. My heart raced. My tears weren't bound like the rest of me, flowing freely down my face. Neither was my mind. I was screaming in my head as the blood ran down the steps of the platform, spreading across the room.

Borger sheathed my dagger into its scabbard, gripped Arnon's wrists, and dragged him out of the stream.

My life with him flashed through my mind. Regret. Love. Rage. I felt it all. I didn't know if my parents were dead or alive. The not knowing helped me fool myself into thinking that perhaps there was a chance I wouldn't have to deal with the grief of their loss.

I wouldn't be able to fool myself about Arnon. The chances I didn't take and the words I didn't say would haunt me forever.

Helstrid knelt beside him, laying his head on her lap. She closed his eyelids, her fingers trailing over his nose and lips like she was the one who had spent a life beside him.

My muscles still ached. I knew that much. I was still under her power, but the sorrow and shock in me merged into rage when her lips touched his. A kiss, gentle at first, then determined, decided. She did what I wasn't able to do.

More than my will to break free, I now wanted to kill her. Not for the kiss, but for robbing me of my chance to tell Arnon the truth. I'd chop her into pieces and feed her to the grayfur-cats that roamed the woods near Heedeon. I'd pour dragonbane in her drink, enough to keep her immobile but not enough to send her into slumber. I'd tie her to the skinner and slice her like a horned rabbit, knowing she felt every stroke of my blade.

The symbol of the winged crown on the surface of the Mezar shone with a golden light. Every carved pattern and rusty corner was illuminated. Small particles ascended from the Mezar, moving like fireflies.

Everything around me fell still. Nothing moved but the lights. A thin line crossed through the air, connecting each particle, forming the symbol of the winged crown above me. Blue skies appeared inside the crown. Birds with golden feathers crossed them. The symbol dispersed, the sky expanding above me.

The gray marble floors were replaced by white stone. I ran my hand across the smooth surface, my reflection staring back at me. My head was shaved, my feet were bare, and my garments were white, embroidered with golden patterns shaped like feathers. A ring was on my finger—two wings joined by a red stone.

I narrowed my eyes, noticing skin stories painted on my head.

A white fountain was to my right. At the center were three statues, each with two wings. They were naked, their feathers laced with one another. A tree sprouted from the center, its roots spilling through the crevices between their hands. Its branches were heavy with sun-kissed apples. The same kind Ma and Da always had in our kitchen. I missed them. I needed them. I needed Arnon.

Gutted and confused, I approached the fountain and sat on its edge as the branches swayed in the gentle breeze. I chanced a look at the water. The skin drawings on my head were gold, their lines sharp and thin.

Twelve large statues served as pillars, upholding a round entablature. They were comprised of six armored men and six armored women facing the horizon. No armor was the same, but they all bore the symbol of the winged crown on their backs.

Another flock of birds crossed the sky, their feathers silver this time, each reflecting the light of the sun. I walked toward one of the statues. No book or dream could have ever prepared me for the sight in front of me.

Waterfalls plunged from the surrounding mountains, creating a river that ran through a white city. Though I was too far up to appreciate every detail of its architecture, I was still able to see how every building was built so trees could grow around them. Branches and roots weren't trimmed or pruned. The city had been adjusted to fit the vegetation as it expanded.

I was strangely calm. Arnon's death was fresh in my mind, but it didn't pain me. It felt like a scarred wound.

Behind me was a temple. Vines grew across its walls and around its columns, carrying flowers in tones of red and gold. A set of stairs led up to its double white doors which nearly reached the ceiling. Two Obsynth guards stood by the steps, holding a spear in one hand and a whip in the other. They were more muscular than the ones from Heelyan, each shielded by bulky armor.

The doors opened and two men walked out, smiling at one another. They resembled those I had seen in a previous vision, naked. One had eyes like gold and hair the color of wheat, twisted back and held together by a thin golden vine. His bearded face was marked with a skin story shaped like a winged dragon. He was broader than the other, the white garment covering his body allowed enough light to reveal his toned legs and the wideness of his chest. The other stood taller, eyes and hair as brown as the bark of a cornelia tree. His garments had a hint of green to them, still almost as white as the man beside him. They laced fingers, talking as they strolled along. They moved through me like the morning mist, continuing toward their destination. I followed them. I could've stayed put and spent time wondering why I was suddenly a ghoul, but they had snagged my curiosity.

They walked past the fountain and the tree, coming to a balcony overlooking the white city. A decanter filled with red wine and two crystal cups were waiting on a table. Their conversation continued as the man with golden eyes poured the wine. Longing marred his face, but there was also a hint of regret.

I tried listening, but their words were mumbles. I tried reading their lips, but I couldn't follow them. The only word I was able to make out was "Peritas."

Their faces grew rigid and cold.

The one with brown hair shifted into a dove and the other into a lion. The lion swallowed the dove, its action causing my surroundings to be engulfed by shadow.

The numbness I felt toward Arnon was gone in an instant. All I could think about was the blade meant to protect me from harm had taken the life of the one who meant the most to me.

CHAPTER ELEVEN

The blink of an eye brought me to a room with walls covered in mildew and iron bars placed over every window. I approached one of the windows. The ocean was outside, meeting gray skies on the horizon. Waves crashed against the outer walls of whatever structure I was in.

"Apologies for my choice of location," said a voice so soothing, I imagined even the most dangerous predator bending to its every word. "But it's finally time for us to talk."

It was the man with golden eyes. He had a gold winged crown on his head, his hair tied back.

"Tell me your name," I demanded, my eyes following the spaulders on his shoulders. They rose to his ears, bending into the shape of wings

"Hanell," he replied.

One expects to feel awe and wonder when standing before one of the gods. I felt rage. No peace. No pain. Just rage.

"You came to solve your own issues?" I asked.

"I did. You're part of the solution. I waited eighteen years for the seed to break ground within Arnon."

The upper left side of his chest was in view, the rest covered by a cloth that seemed to be made of diamonds. A silver kilt draped down his waist, reaching his knees.

"Aren't you a god? Why wait for an innocent to die? Couldn't you have intervened?"

"He isn't dead."

"Not dead..." I mumbled, conflicted if whether I should believe him.

"He's on his quest," he continued.

"Fuck your metaphors. Fuck your issues. Why are you talking to me? Unless all those books are wrong, you created an entire world—another god. Surely, you can fix this yourself."

"Blood speaks louder than power."

"So the Creator has lost power over his own creation," I said. "Is that what you're trying to say? Speak plainly. Or is flowery tongue your way of telling creation you're above us?"

His face flushed and his eyes narrowed. "I didn't lose power. I made a mistake. Love was one of them."

"Do you want the Mezar?" I asked. "Is that what you're after?"

He chuckled. "Even if I did, it would be of no use. I can't open it. But I need to know what lies inside. I need to know what words Lucifer wrote in his epistle."

"Why do his words matter so much?"

"Love fools us into thinking secrets will be kept safe. His epistle is a weapon of revenge. A weapon that's now bound to you." Hanell was a god, but my question was powerful enough to fill him with sorrow. "I can't fight against my own shadow, Bellwound. There are powers that go beyond gods and immortality. I may have created life, but not even a god can control it. You're the in-between. I can't touch him. I can't wound him. I can't live with him. I can't—"

"You love him."

Silence.

"Fallen Stars roam Thestlen again," I said. "I hear he's returning soon. Why not face him yourself? Why rely on me?"

"Love doesn't wither because of betrayal," he said. "It's a power that even holy beings don't fully understand."

"You said I'm the in-between. That I can defeat him. How?"

"Trust me."

"Never," I said. "I trust my truth. I was lied to, betrayed, and now parted from…" The pain was closer than my next breath. "I trust in me. Bellwound Throvar. No one else. I have faith in *me*."

"You can follow him," he said.

My body tensed. "Arnon?"

"You can go to him."

"How?"

"Lay down your life and you'll be reunited. I'll make sure of it."

My feet stumbled back, my hands curling into fists. "Lay down…"

"His quest is not in Thestlen. He didn't choose his course, but

I hope you make the right decision and remain on yours. I will give you more than a quest. I will give you divinity."

"What's that?"

"Power. Enough power to perhaps aid you in traveling between all realms."

"*Perhaps?* Gods don't seem to know much."

"Free will is a strong and unpredictable force, even for us, Bellwound."

"There's something stronger than free will." My chest raised with a breath. "Pain. And I have been living in pain because of your kind."

"I've been in pain for five thousand years," he said.

"Let's say I choose to follow Arnon. How will you discover the truth of the Mezar?"

"Death wouldn't rid you of your purpose, Bellwound."

"So I'd continue on…"

"It would be a different journey, but yes."

"And you could do it now?" I trembled at the sound of my words. "Right here?"

"Yes," he replied without hesitating.

I remembered the dream. I remembered Arnon's eyes meeting mine before Borger tossed him under the flowing blood. Hanell was a god—a creator, but I couldn't trust his words. Who was to say he wasn't manipulating me to do his bidding? At least staying alive in Thestlen meant I'd remain in a world familiar to me.

"Can you take the pain away?" My eyes welled up. "If I choose to stay alive, can you at least do that? I can't bear to see Arnon. To remember the sound of the dagger..."

"If you forget pain, you forget love. And if you forget love, you forget power. But whether you stay alive or lay down your life, it's only through divinity that you'll be able to see him again. The same with your parents."

"You know where they are?"

"With Arnon in the Dark Beyond."

"Dead, then," I said. "Easier to say they're dead, no?"

"But they are not." He tried to lay a hand on my shoulder. I stepped back before he could touch me. He stood in majesty, but his actions were as low as those of thieves. I was a pawn bound to live in the aftermath caused by the mistakes of the gods.

"Can gods die?" I asked. My question was met with a confused stare. "You're telling me I need divinity to have enough power to follow Arnon, my parents, and perhaps defeat Lucifer, correct?"

He frowned.

"Then perhaps divinity will also grant me enough strength to destroy you."

"A mortal defying and threatening me?"

"A god in dire need of a mortal's help?"

Hanell smiled. "You're so much like him. When I first heard it, I didn't think it was possible. How could it be? But seeing you—"

"Fuck your riddles. You'll hold true to your word and grant me divinity because,"—I shrugged—"let's face it, you need me."

He stepped forward, standing only inches away from me.

"When I was born, an echoing prophecy in Valleyner grew into a loud story. The birth of Hanell marked the beginning of a rebellion. I was a lowly young god at the time when I first heard it. I never cared for prophecies, you see. The worst thing about them is the feeling of being imprisoned by a fate you cannot change."

"Why are you telling me this? Do you feel like you owe me an explanation?"

"I owe you a warning. If you are prophecy incarnate, then I'll do what's in my power to eradicate your existence once I'm done with you. There won't be a trace left of your flesh, spirit, voice, or thoughts. Go in peace with my power and you may persist."

"If pain is stronger than free will, Hanell, then it'll be pain that will grant me the strength to destroy you."

Suddenly, I was surrounded by darkness. Was he keeping his word? Was he granting me divinity? Or was I being cast into oblivion like Lucifer?

A mirror appeared before me. I was naked except for the pendant around my neck that was shaped like the winged crown on the Mezar.

Behind me, in the dark, was a pair of scarlet eyes. A white snout crawled out of the shadows. A mane followed, then six wings unfurled. I didn't turn around.

The warmth of the lion's breath touched the nape of my neck. Then it spoke with a voice as low as thunder. "Lucifer and I were like you and Arnon once. We didn't understand our feelings. We were young and full of promise. But it was love that fooled me."

"Do you regret your love for him?"

"I regret making him." He snarled. "I regret making him a lowly god like me. I regret the day I walked through the garden and fell in love with that rose. The white of its petals reminded me of a blank canvas—a chance to start something new. Its stem was thornless. It posed no threat. I didn't have to pluck it. I could've left it there. It would've lived longer. Only I didn't. I put it in a vase and whispered secrets to it day and night. Why did I talk to it? I had no one else. I thought it wasn't listening. It withered, but instead of dying, its petals turned to gold. Gold turned to wings—wings that belong to the Dove, to him. And my love grew each day, but it was love that kept me blind." His scarlet eyes glistened.

I turned around to face him. "Maybe we'd all be better off if you still were, Hanell."

A scarlet tear ran down his face. "Drink it."

I brushed a finger over his cheek, the tear now clinging to my skin, and brought it to my lips. It was sweet at first before turning sour. Then it burned. The heat coated my tongue and moved down, shooting through the rest of my body. My heart pounded. I wanted to jump and fly. I wanted to be in many places at once. Something crawled across my limbs, flowing through my veins, spreading down my feet.

He flapped his six wings toward me and disappeared in a flash of light.

CHAPTER TWELVE

Memory is a strange thing. It vanishes without question and shows up when uninvited. I recalled the day Arnon pushed me into the lake, and I struck my head on the rock. Everything went dark and cold. I remembered opening my eyes as he looked down at me. His face was blurry while I struggled to catch my breath. As air returned to my lungs, my surroundings sharpened, his face in full view.

I felt the same way now. But not only did I struggle to breathe, I struggled to believe I had returned to my nightmare. The room was a blur, but I could still make out the shapes before me. Arnon's body dampened by blood, his head on Helstrid's lap, their lips still locked.

I suddenly felt like I had the strength to move mountains, but my limbs didn't know how to respond. Everyone in the room watched Arnon, Oriah and Loghleen included. The kissing was passionate. Helstrid's tongue was visible as it slid into his mouth. Each chin tilt into him painted red upon her cheeks as her nose grazed his.

His bloody body screamed death, but I chose to cling to Hanell's words that he was alive somewhere.

Arnon groaned with a heaving chest. My body felt numb. The tears stopped streaming from the statue. Helstrid laid his head on the floor and rose to her feet, her face hopeful.

She smiled in awe at Arnon's hastening breaths. Longing was in her eyes when Arnon opened his, now scarlet. He wriggled like a fish out of water, beating himself on the ground.

A Nephilin cried out, "Peritas! Peritas!"

"Peritas!" They all chanted in exclamation.

A tear streamed down Helstrid's face. Borger had on a brooding smile, twirling the dagger in his hand.

Arnon's movements ceased. The room fell quiet.

Helstrid knelt beside him, laying his limp head on her lap again. His eyes stared at nothing, until he blinked.

"Did the Dove keep his promise?" she asked, caressing his cheek. "Did you come back to me?"

"My treasure." Behind every word was a cadence that sounded like Arnon. But the voice didn't belong to him. It was deeper, sounding like someone who had been tortured.

"He did," she said. "You're here, Reemon."

"I am, my darling. Our Dove is faithful."

There was tension in the way they stared at one another. Their eyes alone seemed to beg all in the room to give them privacy. But none obliged. I quivered when they shared an iron-tasting kiss. He grabbed her by the waist, begging her to sit on top of him right on the platform. She did as he requested, helping herself out of heavy, stained clothing. He cupped her breasts, squeezing them like ripe fruits, his pants tightening around him like they once did for me.

The audience wasn't enough to make them stop. The Nephilins were intrigued, almost begging them to continue their burgundy rhythm. Helstrid hastily removed Reemon's clothes. I had imagined Arnon's hard cock for years—and had fought against such thoughts just as often. Watching Helstrid spread her legs and take it inside her made it difficult to remember he was somewhere else. He was not naked, engorged inside a Nephilin, not there for me to see and never touch.

It was still his body, and one I was so close to savagely protecting. It was the body that had swam with me in rivers and gone hunting with me in the cold winter. Every muscle I wanted flexing around me was tightening around the creature who had stolen him away. This was why he had been called the seed of darkness. He had been housing a Fallen Star.

I had something in me now too. I had been given divinity. I assumed I'd only know what that meant if I behaved as recklessly as the gods did. But how?

I wanted to cling to the logical. I needed to believe Arnon was gone, but seeing Reemon using his body to hold Helstrid, the way he dragged his lips across her cheek, forced me to see the one I loved.

I focused on Helstrid. My mind was pulled into hers like a body dragged by a strong current. Images filled my head. The face of a man I had never seen. His brown skin was exposed, covered in silver skin-stories. A ring was in his nose, eyes like honey. Sweat beaded down his brow. He had his hands on her waist. I followed the soft trail of hair on his stomach. He was inside her, lying on top of a pair of gray wings—Reemon's true form.

A scream thrust me out of her mind. Helstrid had fallen over, her trembling hands pressed against the sides of her head.

I tried doing the same to Reemon, but just when the pull began, I was shoved back with a wave of his hand. My back struck the wall, leaving me breathless. Reemon gazed at me like I was a dangerous creature that needed to be squashed quickly. Though his eyes marked me for death, his quivering fists begged for patience.

The other Nephilins muttered amongst each other, gazing at me harder than at the naked subjects in the room.

His body shifted into shadow, engulfing Helstrid and the other Nephilins in the room, leaving Oriah and Loghleen behind. The disembodied form traveled through the air, shattering one of the stained-glass windows as it rushed away.

Shards fell across the floor. I saw my life in them, scattered into small pieces and impossible to put back together.

CHAPTER THIRTEEN

The Mezar was still on the floor, covered in blood. Oriah and Loghleen drew closer as I bent down to retrieve it.

"He came to me," I said with the Mezar in hand. "Hanell. Two seconds too late."

Their faces were shrouded in confusion.

"Came to you?" Loghleen asked. "By the feather, what do you mean?"

"Exactly what I said." My eyes were on the surface of the Mezar, on the blood clinging to the rust, on the symbol smeared in scarlet.

"What did he want?" Oriah asked.

"To talk," I said.

"Bellwound, you must—"

"What else do I have to be?" Oriah fell quiet as my voice boomed across the empty hall. "Who else will lie to me? Who else will use me? The only thing I must do right now is grieve the loss of…" My words broke into sobs, the kind no man, regardless of strength, could stop. I held the Mezar close to my chest, clinging to it as if Arnon was about to crawl out of its crevices. After my body had run out of tears, I took a deep breath. "I'm going to kill him," I whispered.

"Who?"

"Hanell," I said. "I'll destroy him."

"You'll destroy a god?" Oriah frowned.

"He needs me," I said. "He burns to know what's inside this fucking box. He claimed I'm the only one who can open it. How that'll happen, I don't know."

"Remember," Oriah said. "It's not a matter of destroying gods. It's a matter of saving innocent lives."

"Perhaps we can do both. Kill the gods and protect mortals."

They stared like I had lost sight of reason. I didn't care.

"We have to warn someone," Loghleen said. "We have to tell them what we've seen. We need to seek aid."

"Who, my love?" Oriah asked. "Our kind went into hiding thousands of years ago. And the few we just saw are on the wrong side. Who will believe the day of reckoning is here? The Faith are ignorant and remain locked away in their towers in the east, reaping people to join a council that is now fallen. Kings are too consumed with power. The tales of the old immortal crowns are mere fables in the minds of most."

"Those who believe the stories will side with us," she said.

"The problem is that the stories are wrong," I said. "Lucifer and Hanell loved each other. This war wasn't stirred by rebellion and vengeance. It was stirred by love and whatever happened to it."

"How do you know?" Oriah asked.

"I've seen it," I said. "Hanell showed it to me."

Their surprise was evident in their silence.

Loghleen finally pierced the quiet. "A broken heart doesn't know how to measure its actions. But regardless of what the stories say, Lucifer and those with him are here to destroy Thestlen. All must be warned."

"Who's to say Hanell isn't doing the same to his creations?" I asked. "He could be a sadist who enjoys watching the ones he made suffer."

"We can discuss these things as we head out of this place," Oriah said. "Reemon and the others wouldn't just leave us be."

We hurried down a set of stairs at the end of the hall. I thought about telling them of what Hanell had called divinity. How would I explain that I was now able to peer into minds?

We stumbled upon a roofed cloister encircling a garden. The mist wasn't thick enough to conceal the autumn leaves covering the ground. The trees were naked. There was no breeze. All was quiet.

Something lay on the floor ahead. I thought it was a rock until I drew closer. But it was a boy, laying at the foot of a winged statue, his body surrounded by blood. He had a satchel around his shoulder, and his chest was pierced through by an arrow. My gaze followed the freckles on his cheeks, the curls on his head, his chapped lips. He couldn't have been more than five.

I shook the sadness out of my mind.

"How wrong would it be for me to use his satchel to keep the Mezar?" I asked.

"As sad as this sounds," Loghleen said. "He won't be using it anymore."

I slowly reached behind his neck, holding it while grabbing the leather strap. A throbbing pain pierced my head at the touch. Flashes of light coursed through my mind, merging into revealing images: Borger standing with a grin, a clocked bow in his hand; the boy staring from the other side, trying to catch his breath. Shadows. Many Shadows.

"No!" The vision vanished at the sound of my scream.

"What's wrong?" Loghleen asked, alarmed.

"I saw"—I shuddered—"his mind. The last thing he saw..."

Loghleen's face paled. "How is that possible?"

I told them. Though many had kept secrets from me most of my life, I wasn't about to start doing the same. They didn't have to understand. They just needed to know.

"The Mistrid blessing," Loghleen said. "He granted you power."

"Is that what divinity means?" I asked.

"It's a Valleynerian blessing passed down from the Regent, Hanell's parents. No mortal has ever received such a gift."

"Nor any of our kind," Loghleen said.

"When I entered Helstrid's mind," I said. "I saw what I think was a memory. I saw Reemon's true form. And then—"

"She screamed," Oriah said. "But why would they just leave? Sure, you can now see into minds, but they could've..." He trailed off, lost in thought.

"Not only are the tales wrong," Loghleen said. "Some tales were never told, Bellwound."

"There's more to you than meets the eye, Throvar," Oriah said.

I looked at the boy. "Think we'll fight him once he turns into a Shadow?"

"Not only him," Oriah said. "But many others." He knelt beside the boy, removed the satchel from his dead body, and handed it to me.

I reached inside. All the little boy had been carrying was a wooden horse. Its mane and tail were blue, its body brown. Underneath the toy was an inscription: *With love. Da.*

I gently laid the wooden horse on the boy's chest. I didn't care about good and evil. No godly cause mattered to me. The boy's wounds were as deep as my confusion, his bruises as dark as my heart. His little body assured me of one thing—the gods deserved to be punished.

We continued, and I suddenly regretted my every step. The quaint brick homes and cobblestone streets weren't enough to distract me from the mangled bodies. They lay scattered like bloody ornaments meant to adorn Sandrovar.

I was afraid to be the recipient of their last memories. Would they simply come to me as I walked past them? I didn't want to drown in dead memories and waking nightmares at the same time.

I walked past a woman clinging to her child, waiting to see if a memory flashed in my head. Nothing. There was a man with a slit throat, face down on the ground. My mind remained unscathed.

Silence hovered, but the rage—the untamed, wild beast that was present in my every step—now that was as fierce as a waterfall.

Fireplaces still burned inside a few homes. Riders lay near their dead horses. More kids. More men. More women. More innocent lives.

The three of us came upon Sandrovar's stone wall. It rose about fifty feet in the air. Two watchtowers and a bolted iron door lay between them. There was a narrow door at the foot of one of the watchtowers, leading to a round staircase.

Emotion and memory were like wild animals. One assumes they've been tamed, but sooner or later they lash out, embracing their old nature. As we walked up the spiral staircase of a watchtower, I remembered the afternoons Arnon and I spent poring over books. He liked to learn about the wars and history of Thestlen. I preferred legends. But we had always shared one desire—we wanted to see the big castles and cities in the stories for ourselves. Our wish had come true. It was not in the way we expected, but we had seen them together.

As we continued our ascent, screeches and growls traveled through the air, growing louder with our every step. We didn't stop, but we knew what was happening outside. The dead were coming back to life. We emerged on the wall walk, stumbling upon four dead guards. But it wasn't their mangled bodies that held our gaze. It was the city.

I had read about the legends of dragons. I had imagined their roars. The sounds coming from the dead were more frightening than any primal siren my mind could conjure up. Shadows thrashed, coming back to life. Even dismembered limbs crawled around, searching for their owners.

"Bellwound," Loghleen said. "Should your plan to kill the gods succeed, I'll gladly stand beside you. No living creature deserves this."

Oriah rushed to the edge and glanced down. "Can you make it, Bellwound?"

I took a step forward, my ankle grazing the hand of one of the dead soldiers. Oriah was replaced by the image of a Shadow gnawing at the guard's neck. I jerked my ankle away, the vision disappearing immediately.

Reality was once again in front of me. The frightening roars weren't just bellowing from the city. They were now coming from the four thrashing guards on the ground. Their armor rattled against the stone floor, their eyes wide and defiant.

I glanced over the edge of the wall. Maybe I'd make the fall. Maybe not.

A screech sounded from behind me, and I turned. One of the guards—now a Shadow—lunged forward. I leaned back before it could touch me, air replacing the ground beneath my feet. The edge of the wall grew smaller. The sinking feeling in my stomach lasted until my back thudded against the ground. I couldn't breathe. I waited for pain—excruciating pain. But the discomfort I felt didn't match any broken bones or bruised limbs.

I held up a hand. I opened and closed my fingers. My body

had changed. Maybe it was still changing. I didn't know. I stood up as Oriah and Loghleen leapt from the wall, landing effortlessly on their feet.

Loghleen grabbed me by the arm, forcing me up. Luckily, my legs still moved. Oriah grabbed my other arm. They tried to help me move at their pace. But my feet followed by themselves. I shoved their hands away and ran beside them. There was more to divinity—or the Mistrid blessing as they called it—than seeing the memories of the dead after all.

No Shadows pursued us. Their screeches bellowed as we ran through the vegetation. We stopped once the trees paved the way for a cliff overlooking a valley with a river cutting through it.

I opened and closed my hands as if the gesture could answer all my questions. Oriah and Loghleen stared, not saying a word. I also had nothing to offer. I didn't know the extent of what was happening to me. And neither did they.

The screeches of the Shadows howled through the air. I waited for someone to decide our next steps. No one suggested anything. We stayed by the edge of the cliff, silent, resting on the fallen tree trunks until the rage of the Shadows faded into silence.

Night fell. Maybe we were all in a state of shock, trying to find answers. At one point, Oriah crawled next to Loghleen and laid his head on her chest. They were fortunate to have each other. I was more alone than ever.

I trudged through the vegetation, finding a tree so wide, its roots formed a cave broad enough to fit me. I whistled before crawling in, making sure to scare away any lingering critters.

I missed my bed, my home. I missed my parents bickering and Arnon's outrageous ideas, like going fishing in the middle of a rainstorm. The ordinary was desirable and now only attainable in my dreams.

***

Daylight pierced the waning darkness when I woke up. I lay on the dirt, my mind revisiting yesterday's events. I was going to walk back to Oriah and Loghleen, and Arnon wouldn't be around. Starting my first full day without him felt like he was dying before me all over again.

I laid a hand over the satchel, the rough texture of the Mezar still tangible beneath the leather. Touching it tamed my feelings. I felt a numbing peace as my thumb followed the outer rim of the Mezar.

"He's not dead," I whispered, hoping Hanell had been true to his word. "He's not dead."

I crawled out and walked through the woods, where I found Oriah and Loghleen munching on a yellow apple.

"Morning." Oriah pointed left. "Help yourself."

A sun-kissed apple tree stood, its branches hanging low and laden with fruits.

I picked one and slugged my way to the stub of a tree trunk.

"You have every reason to mourn," Oriah said, wiping his lips with the back of his wrist.

"He's not dead," I said sharply, my breath steam.

"But he's not here," Loghleen said. "You can mourn his absence."

"But whilst you mourn," Oriah continued, "we need to decide our next steps."

"Any suggestions?" I sunk my teeth into the apple. "I'm all ears."

"Vragner." Oriah slapped his hands on his thighs and got up. "They have a large army, and they also spread many of the Valleynerian scrolls around Thestlen. The village of Erchmon is on the way. We can stop there for food and shelter."

"So we just show up unannounced and hope they listen?" I asked.

"We have the Mezar," Loghleen said. "And Oriah and I will be proof enough. If there's a kingdom that's always feared Lucifer's coming, it's Vragner. Trust me, they'll listen once they take notice of our eyes."

"And then what?" I asked.

"One step at a time," Oriah said.

CHAPTER FOURTEEN

We walked for three days. Ordinary humans would've needed a week to get as far as we did. The journey gave me time to understand the aftermath of the Mistrid blessing on my body. I'd get tired, but not like before. I'd need food, but not as much or as often as I once did.

The journey also gave me time to dig deep into my mind and try to remember a couple of things Mr. Helvug—or Uncle Pyeus as I always called him—had taught me about Vragner. I didn't have much luck. All I remembered was that it was the first kingdom in Thestlen and a few lost scrolls claimed the Vragnerians learned their construction skills from Stars, the servants of the Creator.

The snow-covered peaks followed us until our arrival in Erchmon at sundown. We found ourselves at the wall that guarded the village—a combination of brick and wood. It was no more than ten feet tall with two watchtowers next to a hoary old gate, both patrolled by two armored guards with spears.

"Who might y'all be?" one of them asked, his armor scarlet.

"Travelers looking for a place to stay," Oriah promptly replied.

"Destination?" asked the other, his armor gold.

"Vragner," Loghleen answered. "We have family there."

"There's talk of strange things brewin' that way," said the one with red armor.

"That's why we want to get there as fast as we can," Loghleen said.

"You lot heard something?" asked the other.

"Nothing of real substance," Oriah replied.

The guard in the red armor stared at Oriah and Loghleen. "Oy, listen," he said. "Your eyes, if they were gems, you'd be able to buy a castle with them. Where you both from?"

"The South." Loghleen's voice never wavered. "We've traveled far to see our family."

"If I were you," the guard in gold started, "I'd sell those eyes. Better blind and rich than poor and pretty, huh?" He nudged his companion.

The guards broke out into laughter. Oriah and Loghleen weren't amused. My patience waned.

"You still need to see our overseer," said the soldier in scarlet after catching his breath. "All outsiders do. I'm sure you're alright with that."

"We'll do as you please," Oriah said.

"Wait there," said the guard in gold. "I'll lead you in."

The wooden gate creaked open. The tiled-roof homes were

painted in bright shades of green, yellow, and red. The little stores selling pastries, vegetables, and spices made the village feel warm and welcoming. But the faces of those on the street told a different story.

I didn't need powers to notice the discomfort in the people we passed. They were like a crowd ready to watch an execution. They stopped whatever they were doing to observe us walk by. Oriah and Loghleen were uncomfortable, perhaps because they already stood out from most people. Nephilins had a way about them. Their walk was poised, and they never slouched, unlike humans.

We approached what I would've assumed was just another ordinary house, had it not been for the scarlet banner with a sword and rose stamped on it. Its edges were tattered, the dangling threads moving in the breeze. The guard remained nameless. I expected him to say something up until the moment he led us to the stone steps and through the doors, but he kept to himself.

Two guards stood by the doorway behind us. There was a man on a chair, dressed in red robes. The pauldrons on his shoulder were gold, linked to each other by a chain running over his chest. His face was flushed. He dangled a gold cup from one hand, clinging to a bottle of red wine with the other. A young man was to his right and a girl to his left. They couldn't have been more than twenty.

"Brave of ye to 'ere come," he said, taking a sip from his drink. "Ye not heard de' stories? There was some disaster in Sandrovar. They deserved it though. Never aided none in war. Lazy little fuckers."

"Can he even make a conscious decision about who we are?" I asked.

"I heard that!" He tossed the cup of wine on the floor and slapped the arm of the boy next to him. "Pick that up, ye imbecile, or I'll have my way with ye later. By a serpent's eye! Can't do ye'r job. I must do evr'thin' he'."

His accent was perhaps Metranian, like Atholeeon, but not as strong. He stared at the three of us, his fingers crawling through his beard—which looked like woven vines. "Where ye off to?"

"Vragner," I said before anyone else could answer. Yes, he was drunk, but Oriah and Loghleen's eyes still made a statement. I wanted to draw as much attention away from them as possible.

"What's leading ye there?" He took a gulp from the wine.

"Family."

"Yers?" He pointed at Loghleen. "'Cause it's clear ye are not related to t'ose two."

"Yes," I said. "Mine. They're helping me find my way back."

"Why wander so far if ye didn't know how to return?"

"We don't mean to be rude," Loghleen said. "But the boy's parents died in the Sandrovar attack. We survived. Now we're taking him home."

"Sad to hear." He nodded, eyes staring into the distance. "It's even sadder dat I have to pretend to care. I've to sit on this damn chair and listen to traveler's stories. I fought for Vragner, ye know? I gave up my Metranian loyalty and became a Vragnerian. Their ways always appealed to me. Like a serpent attacks a bird, I fought hard for them lot. And for what? To sit on this fuckin' chair. Curse the gods and the mortals and anything dat walks."

"The stories you've heard," Oriah said. "I assume they were about war."

"Yes." The man chugged from the bottle. "War and grief and pain. Those Vragnerians then summon my men and my women fit to fight. They claim t'ese attacks are pavin' de way for Lucifer. One was bold enough to say de dead fight for t'ose t'at attacked Sandrovar. I give no fucks if t'e stories are true. How dare t'ey leave me, Kunkard, be'ind? I'm old but not a fool. Curse t'eir beards and bellies and 'usbands and wives!"

"I'm sorry," I said. "Truly."

"T'ese villages are seens as chicken coops to dem, ye see." He grabbed the arm of his wooden chair and managed to stand, wobbling back and forth. "Dey feed us and get us all juicy so we can die first. But dey wan' the young men and women. Dose are importan' to them. Fuck de young. Fuck everyone. How dare dey summon my son and dau'ter?" He fell back on his chair, his body sliding forward. "My son and dau'ter." He beat a fist to his chest. "My son and dau…" He wept.

One of the guards behind us cleared his throat. "What shall we do with them, Lord Overseer?"

"Take 'em to an inn or somefin'. I don't care." He waved us away. "Give 'em swords, too. T'ey look defenseless. T'ey don't seem to know this land. I'll live to see t'ese dark days as an ol' man while my kids die on a battlefield." He slapped the arm of the girl beside him. "More wine, you dumb whore!" He beat a fist on the arm of the chair.

"Yes, of course." The girl shivered.

We were sent off to the sound of his low sobs. One of the guards in the room led us to an old inn, The Furry Eagle. Oriah had some coin and used it to book two rooms for the night. Mine wasn't the most spacious, but at least I'd have a bath before sleeping on a bed.

The chatter, laughter, and music of the downstairs pub leaked into my room. I tried to peer into pubgoers' minds. I wanted to make sure picking up random unwanted thoughts without intent wasn't a skill I had picked up with the Mistrid blessing. To my relief, I couldn't see into their heads. It was in the disturbing quiet that my thoughts found room to wander. I was able to break my way into Helstrid's thoughts without laying a finger on her. Perhaps I didn't need to touch things to see into them. Still, there was no rhyme or reason to it.

A merry melody traveled from the pub into my room. But no laughter came from me. It tied a knot in my throat instead. "The Merry Tidings of Swords and Kings" was Arnon's favorite song request at Mr. Octern's pub. Whenever we were there for a drink, he'd ask for the song.

Clash and clang be music to the ears

Of conquerors, wanderers, and kings

Though they remind the ordinary folk

That death is no tale of old

They turn ordinary boys into kings

Dancing and music follow the sounds of gore

Sparking hope that faith lives forevermore

Merry tidings from the swords of steel

That make all rebels kneel

The happy song brought on dark thoughts. If I touched Arnon's body, would I be able to see into Reemon's mind or would I see Arnon's tormented thoughts in the Dark Beyond? Would I see his very last memory before he was stabbed? Or worse, would I know the truth of his feelings for me?

ORIAH

CHAPTER FIFTEEN

"They're staring," Loghleen said.

"Let them." I sipped from my wine. "It's a pub. I'm sure they've seen much worse. If they end up bothering us, we can use the swords they brought over."

She briefly smiled at my comment.

"You're lost in thought," I said.

"Hanell came to him." She held my hand. "Spoke to him. Blessed him."

"And he can now see the memories of the dead. There's so much we didn't know."

"And so much we do. Did you expect Seaahra and Stenan to conceal so much from him?" she asked.

"Can you blame them?"

She let go of my hand at my question.

They had always been adventurous, daring. They were always ready to aid Loghleen and me after we left Sandrovar. Most Council members opposed our presence back then. They paved the way for them to accept us into the castle.

"We all have our burdens to carry," Loghleen said. "We've been carrying ours for a long time."

"Do you serve Hanell?" I asked.

"No." She sniggered. "You?"

"No. Neither do I serve Lucifer. I serve mortals, like Bellwound. I don't want to be a pawn in the game of the gods."

"We're a bit late for that."

A boy sat a few tables away, his staring noticeable under his brown hood.

"Do you ever regret our decision to leave Sandrovar?" I asked, trying to disregard him.

"It's not regret." She glanced around the pub. "It's the notion that we were born into darkness. It's the constant thought that we're evil, that our nature is wicked, and that Helstrid and Reemon taught us our sole purpose was to serve Lucifer. I still struggle with those memories. And hearing Bellwound talk of Hanell's blessing, his love for Lucifer..."

"I wish life had given us peace over war. When I realized I was in love with you, I'd dream of the two of us living somewhere where no one knew who we were. A place where this haunting darkness didn't exist."

"I wished for the same the first time I realized you loved me." She smiled, recalling the memory. "The lake in those caves... I had never seen you look at me that way before."

The boy on the other side folded his arms, eyes still on me.

"Someone is staring a bit too much," I said. "Behind you."

"Do we know them?" She didn't look back.

"I've never seen him in my life."

He got up, letting his hood fall back. His skin was brown and his eyes as yellow as the autumn leaves. His clothes were tattered, and the leather satchel on his shoulder was worn-out. His chest puffed as he determinedly approached, his black curly hair bouncing.

"Mind if I join you?" he asked, his voice never wavering.

"Why not?" Loghleen spread out her hands, inviting him to sit.

He dragged over a chair from the table beside ours. He kept the back of the chair toward us, sitting with his legs spread wide, arms thrown over the chair's top rail.

"How may we be of service?" I asked.

"You always talk like you belong in some old sonnet?" he said.

Who was this kid?

"Do you like stories?" he continued.

"What was that?" I asked. Perhaps the boy was drunk.

"You like stories?" he repeated haltingly.

"Good ones." Loghleen drank more wine.

"You'll love this one then. I turned eighteen a few weeks ago. People from my neck of the woods don't care for birthdays or Blood-dates or whatever you want to call the day I popped out of my mother. I woke up and my uncle Trun was dead. My entire house was destroyed. I never heard anyone come in. By the dragon,

I thought I had gone mad. Thought maybe I was dreaming—"

I shifted in my seat. "Why are you telling—"

"You always interrupt storytellers?"

"Did no one teach you manners, boy?" Loghleen curled her hands into fists.

"I wouldn't get on her nerves if I were you," I said.

He stared, knowing he was wrong but filled with too much pride and ale to apologize.

"Continue," I said.

"I thought I was dreaming. I thought maybe I had too much to drink the night before. But the blood made it all real." He lifted the satchel from his shoulder. "I grabbed this from him. He was holding on to it. And I found"—he slides a box resembling the Mezar over—"this strange box with these patterns and this—"he stabbed a finger over the symbol of the winged crown "—this symbol."

"And what of it?" Loghleen's thumb followed the outer rim of her cup.

"What of it? I then see this thing in my head. Maybe a dream or… I don't know. Two winged men fucking. The man with gold eyes tells me you'd be here. The both of you. Two *Nephilins*. 'Look for the diamond eyes,' he said. And that I had to wait here until your arrival."

I despised the notion of Hanell speaking of my kind—no matter how twisted we were. Maybe he had forgotten the shame he inflicted on my people. But I surely hadn't.

"What's your name?" I asked.

"Kymer Strum."

"Where do you come from, Kymer?" Loghleen asked.

"Dragonhall."

"The land of dragons near Watersong," I said, drinking my wine. "You've journeyed far."

"I took a ship and sailed north of the River Pentan. I've been here since, staring at the face of every single person who walks in this place. And I've never seen eyes as blue as yours. So tell me, why did I have to find you?"

Silence.

"My uncle dies. Then I see two winged men going at it. I'm told you'd be here. And here I find you."

"You have a lot of nerve, Kymer Strum," Loghleen said. "What makes you think we'll talk?"

"Because I know what you are," he said.

"You! You t'ere!" someone shouted.

"What do you want to know?" I asked, noticing Kunkard sitting a few tables to the right.

He waved. "A word, please!"

"I'll leave you be." Kymer grabbed his satchel and tossed it over his shoulder. "I know you won't run. I can see in your eyes that you're as curious as me now. See you in the morning at sunrise? Same place?"

"We'll be here," I said.

He headed up the stairs leading to the rooms on the second floor.

"I'm going to bed," Loghleen said. "I've had enough for one day. I can't take that drunk right now, no matter how sad his story may be."

"I'll be up soon, my darling."

"Goin' to keep me waitin'?" Kunkard shouted as Loghleen made her way up the stairs. "Fuckin' people."

I walked toward him, my cup of wine in hand.

"I won't se' I'm surprised to find ye here," he dawdled. "It's eit'er t'is inn or t'e ot'er one at t'e end of t'e road. And t'at one is pure bird shit. At least ma' men had t'e courtesy of bringing you lot here."

"And for that I am grateful."

"What was t'at 'bout? You have men and women fighting over ye?"

"The boy thought we were someone else."

"Ah, sit." He slowly pulled out a chair. "Sit, sit, sit." He tapped on the wooden seat. "Entertain me a bit."

"What brings you here tonight, my Lord?"

"T'e same t'ing t'at brought me here yesterday. The same t'ing that'll bring me hea' tomorrow."

"No one ever sent word on how your children are doing?"

"T'ey are probably dead," he said. "T'ey called t'e best to Vragner. If t'ey ain't dead, t'ey'll die in some war soon. And now with t'is attack in Sandrovar, t'ey'll be sending men and women everywhere. T'e part t'at is fucked up is t'at t'ey keep using t'ese stories about Fallen Stars and t'e Creator and whatnot to do t'eir bidding. 'Side wit' us and you'll be given titles and land and gold.' T'ey just need a good fuck, if ye ask me. Easier to blame some old tale conjured by the Fait' t'an to see t'e world for what it is. Rotten, if you ask me."

"Do you know who or what killed the people in Sandrovar?" I asked.

"A survivor showed up after ye lot left." He sat up straighter, suddenly lucid. "A boy. No older t'an ten, ye see. He spoke of an army of dead men and women. Maybe it was t'e shock in 'im. Maybe he spoke the trut'. He also brought up somefin' about seeing t'ose with eyes so blue, t'ey looked like ice."

"Did he now?" I shuddered.

"I was never one to read t'e stories, my good man, but I remember a few parts. The Nep'ilins, t'e children of t'e Fallen Stars and 'umans. Dey could only be hurt or killed wit' a blade—a very specific one at that. Ot'erwise, dey'd live forever. Never aging. Frozen at t'irty-t'ree." He chugged down the rest of his drink. "And den… den I saw you hea' and noticed yer eyes. Bluer dan anyt'ing I've ever seen."

"Scary stories for children, my Lord," I said.

"And w'at if t'at's w'at t'ey want us to believe? T'at t'ese stories have not'ing to t'em. And t'en ye realize t'ey were real all along. I could easily believe t'em now."

"I'm going to retire, if you don't mind." I stood. "We'll be on our way tomorrow. If I don't see you, thank you for your hospitality."

"I probably won't even remember ye." He shrugged. "G'night."

We needed to leave. The attacks were giving legs to the stories. Just like him, many would remember them when they saw us. I felt the eyes of those at the pub buried in the back my neck as I walked past them to take the stairs. They were curious, afraid, threatened.

Loghleen sat on a settee by the window in our room dressed in a white linen nightdress, staring at the people walking by on the street.

"He let you go so soon?" she asked.

"Thankfully, he was too drunk to carry a long conversation. And where did you get that nightdress?" I approached her.

"I asked a servant out in the hall for one. They had a spare from a guest who left it here and never returned."

"Kunkard asked about my eyes." I laid a hand on her shoulder, following her neckline, my gaze shifting to her breasts.

"Most of the people in that pub were doing the same," she said. "The boy, Kymer, now his words concerned me. Do you think he spoke true?"

"His tale matched Bellwound's vision." I took off my shirt and walked to the bed, sitting on its edge. She joined me. "And to think—" My words halted when her fingers started tracing me in my pants, keeping up with where I grew. She pulled my head back so our eyes locked.

"I'm done talking war and grief tonight." Her lips brushed mine. One of her arms slipped out of the nightdress. "I just want you," she said, looking down where she captured me. "I want this in me." She placed one of my hands between her legs. She let go of my hand with a shudder once my fingers found their way inside her.

She smelled like a field of honey-daisies—the rarest of all flowers. My mouth yearned to be between her legs. She tasted sweet, like honey. But though we were with each other, I sensed an unsaid distance. Something haunted her mind.

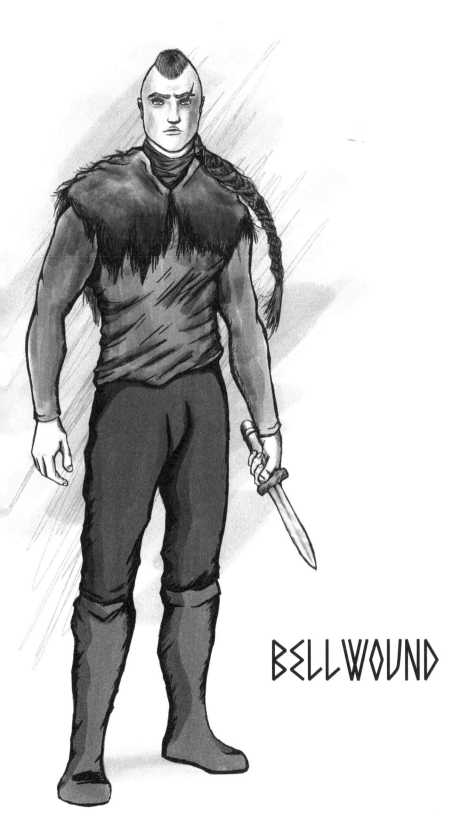

BELLWOUND

(HAPTER SIXTEEN

I wandered the cobblestone streets of Erchmon before the sun rose. Every window was dark, every house quiet. The trees rustled in the cold chill and, occasionally, I'd hear a crow caw or wings flutter.

No sleep found me in the night. The Mezar remained close, always in reach. When I was lying down, it was beside me. When I wandered my room, it was in my grasp. It helped with the grief. It couldn't speak, but holding it brought the same calm Ma's voice did when I was young.

The guard at the east gate was fast asleep, which made walking out easier than expected. After walking through the pine trees, I came across a cliff. Though it was still dark, the faint light of the moon reflected on the river in the distance.

My hands followed the leather strap of my satchel, crawling into its pouch. I ensnared the Mezar and brought it into view. My thumb grazed the etched wings of the crown symbol, the rough texture sending my heart racing. Power. Rage. Sorrow. I felt it all at once.

My mind went dark though my surroundings were still in view. I could touch the trees, walk to the edge of the cliff in front of me, but the images haunting my mind felt more real.

Hanell and Lucifer were on a bed, naked, their bodies glistening with sweat. Lucifer pressed Hanell's head into a pillow while thrusting inside him. Hanell's wings were at ease beside him, the feathers spread out on top of the bed. Lucifer's were pressed against his back, trembling with the back-and-forth movements of his hips.

Lucifer wrapped his arms around Hanell's waist as they both moaned with pleasure. Lucifer's thrusting grew faster. He sank his teeth into Hanell's muscular shoulder blade—a gentle bite filled with pleasure. Biting turned to kisses that ran up Hanell's neck.

Moans shifted into low grunts. Lucifer's hips followed their cadence, the thrusting growing faster and faster until a decisive moan ordered Lucifer's hips to a stop, wings unfurling at his sides.

"I love you," Lucifer whispered in Hanell's ear.

"I love you," Hanell said as Lucifer pressed his chest to his back.

Lucifer lay beside him, pushing Hanell's golden hair out of his eyes. Desire shrouded their faces.

"Wine?" Hanell kissed Lucifer's forehead.

"Always."

Hanell's body resembled a sculpture covered in skin stories. Horses, dragons, winged beings—they were all a part of his body art.

A decanter and two golden grails sat on a corner table. He approached and poured the wine without haste.

"The audience with my parents is tomorrow," Hanell said, returning to bed, handing one of the grails to Lucifer.

"And we're going through with the plan?"

"Our plans haven't changed, even if Valleyner has."

"So we're defying the Regent." Lucifer smirked. "We're defying your parents."

"I may be one of the lowly gods," Hanell said. "But I am still a god."

"And your sister?" Lucifer asked.

"She's my concern," Hanell replied.

"Peritas." Lucifer raised his grail.

"Peritas," Hanell whispered.

Lucifer's lips touched the rim of the grail.

"I know it's a pretty sight," said a voice I didn't recognize. "But you've been staring at the horizon for a long time now."

The image shattered into pieces that drifted into the air, vanishing from sight.

I turned, startled. There stood a boy with brown skin and eyes as bright and yellow as summer apples.

"I guess I'm not the only one who enjoys being alone this early," I said, noticing the satchel around his broad shoulders.

"Kymer," he said.

"Bellwound."

"And what's that in your hand?" he asked.

My chest tightened. "Family heirloom."

"Looks interesting."

"What brings you to the very popular village of Erchmon, Kymer?" I tucked the Mezar back into my satchel.

"Fate," he replied.

"Fate?"

"I don't believe in coincidences. Never did. I'm from Dragonhall. My people believe the first dragon that crosses your path in life, no matter how big or small, is yours to care for. No dragon is a coincidence. No encounter is without purpose."

"You've seen dragons?" I asked, struggling to contain my excitement.

"I've ridden them," he said proudly.

"By the dragon." I scratched the back of my head. "I hope I get the chance to see one. I've always loved the stories of the dragon riders."

"We've trained them to stay near Dragonhall. Many hunt them for their horns and claws and hide. They don't fly far. Well, most don't. You always get a rebel here and there."

"And you have one?" I asked. "A dragon?"

"I do," he said behind a smirk. "Well, I did." A hint of sadness followed his words. "It returned to the wild when I decided to venture this far."

"And you've journeyed this far simply because of fate?"

He stared into my eyes. "Are you hungry? We could go to a pub for breakfast. Talk about travels and dragons. The braid and the shaved sides of your head—Metra?"

"Heedeon," I said. "Close enough."

"Oh, I've heard of your horned rabbits." He laughed.

"The tales are true."

"So, breakfast?" he insisted. "I'm staying at the Furry Eagle."

"Me too," I said. "The pub downstairs?"

"Yes. Are you walking back now? We could go together."

"No, I'm staying for a little longer."

"I'll head back. Freshen up. See you soon."

"See you," I said.

He glanced over his shoulder three times before disappearing into the trees. He had a way about him—the way he walked and talked. He was confident, but not arrogant. There was wisdom in his words, wisdom peppered with rebellion.

"He's handsome," said a sultry voice so close to my ear, it sent the hairs on my arm into a frenzy. Next to me was a human-shaped shadow without features. "You're enjoying holding on to something of mine, aren't you?" he whispered as I stepped away in haste.

"You're him." I was thankful my heart wasn't the one doing the talking. Otherwise, I'd be screaming.

"You can say my name."

"Lucifer," I said.

"Now, now, I heard you've spent some time with Hanell since your Blood-date. I won't judge you for that. My better half may have granted you the Mistrid blessing, but you're still mine."

"Yours…"

He hovered closer. I inched back.

"It's a sad thing to be lied to," he said. "I was for thousands of years. Much like you. Only I was lied to by my light. My Pale Lion. I was his shadow. His whispers made me and yet he resented me in front of the courts and servants and kingdoms. But the best way to destroy an artist is to taint their art. Humans are his paintings, and I am the black ink."

"Why are you here?" I asked. "*How* are you here?"

"Because of you." He hovered closer. "Since your Blood-date, the longer you live, the stronger I get. You deserve the truth. You were made for it. I can sense the Mezar taking hold of you, and the more it does, the more I become."

I gripped the satchel, clutching the box between my thigh and palm.

His laughter made my blood boil. Were he not a shadow, I would've struck him with a fist.

"I see I'm not wrong. I fashioned the Mezar after all."

"I don't trust the truth of the gods," I said. "Yours or Hanell's. I saw the two of you. Your precious Pale Lion shamelessly showed me."

"I'm not shy, little Bellwound. The Mezar will also show you things. That's how I made it."

"Just spill it." Dawn appeared behind the mountain range on the horizon. "What do you want?"

"We need each other. You may not believe the truth of the gods, but it's a truth you'll never run from. It's in your blood."

"On the contrary, *little* Lucifer." A ferocious growl escaped the shadow. "Hanell needs me to open the Mezar. Something tells me you also need me around. Otherwise, you would've killed me already. But I have no need for either of you."

"Hanell and I share the same cause. I, too, need you to open the Mezar, though I am its maker. It was his curse that bound your mortal life to *my* immortal device. Only, he wants it open so he can destroy it. I want it open to protect it."

"Dragonshit," I said. "All of it. I'm not bound to anything, especially anything you'd protect."

"I can find you in death and in life," he said. "But the others, the mortals, the humans, they'll keep turning into Shadows. I'll keep killing one by one until you do as you're told."

"What if I die before I open this thing?" I asked. "What if neither of you get what you want?"

"I'll say it again. I can find you in death. Just as I've found little Arnon."

A knot formed in my throat. A gripping pain in my chest.

"I thought you didn't trust the truth of the gods," Lucifer said snidely.

I despised him. I despised Hanell. They weren't worthy of stories or songs. I decided to do whatever was in my power to avoid victory for both. Though he was a shadow, faceless and void, his edges shivered as I rushed to the edge of the cliff.

"What if I jump?" I shouted. "What if I die? Yes, you can find me in death, but perhaps I can also destroy you in it."

"While alive, you can open the Mezar and join my cause without eternal punishment. You die without showing me your allegiance and you will be tortured throughout all the ages of this world. And you'll still have to open my device." The sun was rising. "I am still a god." The brighter the sky turned, the fainter his shadow grew. "I admire your courage, little Bellwound. But perhaps you need a reminder that gods create and gods destroy. Fight all you want. Help them however you like. But keep on resisting, and I swear that my servants will spare no one. I have spies in every corner. One is inside that village right now."

Distant roars echoed. I recognized them. "Shadows," I whispered.

"You didn't think you were spared in Sandrovar for no reason, did you? We're entangled. Let me offer you some advice. Shadows can't distinguish who you are from the others. I hope today teaches you a lesson since the dead in Sandrovar weren't enough to help you see reason. Every single death today is blood on your hands."

He disappeared, along with the night. The orange hues of dawn were on display beyond the mountains.

I ran back to the village, through the pines, past the sleeping guard, and down the cobblestone streets. I rushed inside the inn and knocked on the door of Oriah and Loghleen's room.

"Open up! Open—"

"By the feather! What is going on?" Oriah answered with a cup of black seed in hand. He noticed the fear on my face.

"Shadows," I said. "They're—"

Screams bellowed from the street. Wailing. Distant growls. Loghleen rushed to the window of their bedroom, her eyes widening. "They're here."

Oriah dropped the cup on the floor. Loghleen leapt across the room, grabbing her sword. Oriah did the same. Two Shadows broke through the window. They each picked one to fight. I stood rooted to the spot while Oriah tried a slash. He missed. Loghleen attempted the same, but the Shadow swayed right. My mind was drawn to theirs though my body wanted to fight them.

I focused on one—the Shadow shaped like a man. His last memory found my own. I didn't need to touch them to see it. I just had to focus. I had done it before. A fireplace, a table, and Helstrid. He screamed louder and louder, my chest tightened at his torment. Anger sprung in me at the sight of the smirk on her face. The faster my heart raced, the fainter the memory grew—until it exploded.

The Shadow plunged to the floor, turning to ash. I thrust myself into the memories of the other—a woman, protecting herself and her child while running through flames. My anger shattered the memory. The Shadow burst into dust.

"How?" Loghleen asked. "How?"

"If I destroy their last memory, they disappear," I said, stunned.

I rushed to the window. Growls and screeches became one with the people's despair. The narrow street swarmed with Shadows. I projected myself into one thought, a man being stabbed. Then to another, a child being burned. I kept on entering their minds, but not fast enough to protect the villagers. When suddenly, I was pulled out of my wandering, unable to tap into their minds.

"What, you're just going to watch people die on the street?" I followed the somewhat familiar voice. Kymer was at the door, chest heaving.

"What're you doing here?" Oriah asked.

"I know exactly who you are. I know what you carry." He reached into his satchel and revealed a box like the Mezar. "I also carry my burden."

"A Mezar?" I asked.

"I don't know what it's called. But I know it cost the lives of people I love. And I refuse to just sit around. So tell me, what are you all doing here? Why do you have that box?"

Another Shadow jumped through the window. I tried to enter its mind, but it was as if I had never done it before. Its cold hands grabbed my neck, sending me to the ground. There was blood on its lips.

I tried to pierce its mind again. Nothing.

Loghleen sunk her blade into its chest. The creature burst into ash.

"I couldn't see it anymore," I said, dusting the ash off my chest. "I couldn't…" I turned to Oriah. "He came to me," I revealed, surveying their faces. "Lucifer. This morning, he came to me. He said there's a spy here. We can't—"

Three Shadows barged through the doorway. Oriah shoved me to the side and swung his sword at one of them. Loghleen leapt on top of the other. The remaining creature shoved Kymer to the side and darted my way. It grabbed me by the arm. I jerked it free, but then it ensnared the other, pulling me to its defiled lips. A burning pain shot down my arm as its putrid teeth sank into my skin.

The creature became deranged as my blood trickled out of the bite. It chanced another.

I had never been thrown in a fire before, but I had been so close to a flame that my skin begged for distance. The bite felt ten thousand times worse.

I went from burning to feeling nothing.

Darkness.

***

The stench forced me to open my eyes, like cracked eggs that had been left out in the sun too long. My chest was bare. My legs were submerged in brown water. The sun struggled to break through the gray. The trees rose so high they seemed to be begging for a way out of this place.

"Bellwound!" The familiar voice stole my breath away. My head jolted in his direction. His chest was exposed, and so were the wounds the dagger had carved into it. He trudged toward me, grabbing branches to pull himself along faster. I did the same, hoping the speed I had gained with the Mistrid would help me, but here—wherever *here* was—I was as slow as my old self again.

His eyes glistened. I could see them in the distance. My heart pounded as we neared each other. Was he real? Was this a dream? I noticed the markings on his body, thin gray lines stretching all over him, like lightening in a storm. He reached forward. I grabbed his hand and pulled him to me. His face burrowed between my neck and shoulder. I wrapped my arms around him.

"By the dragon," I said between heavy breaths. "You're here. You're real."

Hanell hadn't lied.

"So are you," he said, his embrace firmer. "How? I feel like I've been here for weeks. This place… It's…"

I kissed his cheek. "Weeks?" I did it again. "It's felt like an eternity to me." My hand gently turned his face to mine.

I trembled. We'd never been this close before. I could see the steel of his eyes, but also the hints of silvery white in them. Our chests had never pressed this hard against one another. I cupped his face between my hands. He didn't hesitate, grabbing my waist and pulling me harder against him.

"If this is a dream," I whispered, our lips grazing. "If this is death, then I don't want to wake."

"This is no dream, Bellwound. No matter how dark. You don't have to wake. But if you choose to, please… please kiss me before you go."

The tips of our noses touched, like lovers holding hands. My heart had a will of its own suddenly. Our lips brushed. They were shy at first, meeting for the first time. Then there was intent. It didn't take long for our tongues to dance. His hand pressed hard on the nape of my neck. My arm was around him, begging his waist to remain close to mine. I didn't know if we were going to be parted again. I wanted to make up for all the years we had lost at once.

He had tears on his face after our lips parted from one another. Were they tears of regret? What was behind them?

"I've been wanting this for a very long time," he said. "But I was so scared."

"And you think I didn't?" I said with a soft chuckle.

He held my hands, his eyes never leaving mine. "Now I'll never wonder about our first kiss." He kissed the top of my hand. "But I'll always wonder what it would've been like if we had enjoyed a full life together." He led my hand to the wound on his chest. "But I *am* dead, Bellwound. They promised me you'd visit before…"

"Before what?" I gripped his shoulders. "Before what, Arnon?"

"Our journeys started together. But now I need to go on alone."

"I must be dead too, then," I insisted, my eyes jolting to my shoulder, expecting to see the Shadow bites. But there was nothing. "It bit me."

"I don't think you are," he said, puzzled. "Look at me, the markings. And you—"

"Have none," I said.

"It's strange being here." A thin smile took his lips. "Time goes by fast and slow. I feel like I just arrived, but I'm also lingering."

"What's this journey you're talking about?" I asked. "Don't leave me in the dark."

"I have to." His voice broke. "I have to." He kissed me. "I have to." And again. "They kept their promise to me. I need to keep mine."

"What promise, Arnon?" I held his face between my hands. "What are you talking about? We're here and you can't tell—"

"Peritas," he whispered sadly.

"Pe…" My breaths were heavy. "Why are you saying that?"

Golden particles of light emerged from the brown waters of the bog. They hovered in the air like fireflies. "Why did you say that?" I insisted, their numbers growing with my every breath. It didn't take long for me to feel like I was surrounded by a starry sky.

"I'll find you," I said, Arnon's face still between my hands. "I'll find you. I'll come for you." A few of the lights landed on my arms, growing into thin stretching lines. "I don't care where you are. I'll find you."

He gave me a sad smile, a quiet goodbye.

"I *will* come back." The lights grew stronger, hiding him from sight. "I will come back!" I shouted. "I promise. I will find you."

CHAPTER SEVENTEEN

I was warm, suddenly too warm. My eyes fluttered open. A fire. Trees. Flurries. The wild. I lay on top of an animal's pelt. A crow-bear, perhaps? I tried getting up, but my shoulder stung, forcing me to stay put.

I gripped the furry texture, wishing *this* was the dream. My wish wasn't granted. The snow grazed my face as I stared at the gray through the canopy. The trees were naked, ready for winter. So was my heart, stripped from everything I held dear, exposed to the cold.

I was used to rage and sorrow forming an alliance in my mind. Now confusion had joined the war. Had I seen Arnon? Was it a dream? All I had were questions and more questions.

"You shouldn't move," Oriah said in a hoarse voice, his face covered in cuts and bruises. "You were hurt." He sat on the ground, Loghleen beside him. Kymer was on the other side, eyeing me like I was prey. They looked defeated and tired.

"Where are we?" I asked, struggling to break my mind free of the dream. "What happened?"

"We're by the shores of the River Pentan," Loghleen replied. "About a mile east of Erchmon." Her lip was cut. She had a scratch stretching from her cheek down her neck. "You've been asleep for a little over a day."

"A day?" I asked.

"Yes." Kymer walked my way with a hood over his head, his tattered coat smeared in blood. "We thought you were gone."

I stared a little too long at his clothes.

"What happened?" I insisted.

"You were bitten by a Shadow—" Loghleen started.

"I remember that."

"We fled after. We needed to get you help. We made it to the front gate of the village and ran for as long as we could. Oriah carried you, and I had Kymer."

"And the people of Erchmon?"

"Help came," Oriah answered. "But not soon enough to save them."

"So they all died," I whispered.

Rustling footsteps approached from the left. "Let those who came to help speak," a new woman said. She was accompanied by a man, heavy armor shielding their bodies. Crystal, perhaps? Even without the sun, their armor glistened with a soft iridescent hue—like hovering rainbows sparkling with their movements.

"You should thank Myrr here," Kymer said with a frown. "If it wasn't for her, you'd probably be dead."

"Myrr?" I was confused.

"A pleasure, Bellwound." The woman held a fist to her heart. One of her eyes was gray and the other green. The texture of her hair reminded me of Arnon's, only it was brown, like the bark of a bitterlie tree. "And this is Quivern."

"Thank you," I said. "For whatever it is you did."

"You almost died," Quivern said in a gravelly voice. "You would've become one of them. See that tree?" He pointed behind me. "See the vines wrapped around it? That's elemeanor. Mix it with water, and it stops a Shadow wound from festering. Valleynerian medicine. We were lucky to escape. The entire village was destroyed."

His head was bald, and his face was covered in thin scars, like scratches that had aged with time. One was above his left eyebrow, like mine. Skin stories crawled up his neck, the lines not enough for me to discern the image. But it wasn't so much his face or features, but his armor that held my interest.

"It's onovine." Myrr noticed my distraction. "Valleynerian hosts use it for armor and weapons."

"What are you?" I asked.

"There are Stars," Quivern said. "There are Fallen Stars, and then there are those who rebelled way before Hanell and Lucifer declared war against one another. We call our people the Broken— or the Sindal in Thestlenian tongue. We didn't take sides when Valleyner's allegiance was split. We had already been independent before everything happened, respected by the Regent."

"How'd you find us?" I asked.

"Your Blood-date was watched not only by the Council," Myrr said, "but by other forces. How do you think the breomers found you in Heelyan?" She smirked.

"You sent them?" Oriah asked.

"By not taking sides with Hanell, Lucifer, or the Regent," Quivern said, "we were able to free our minds, to study other arts and abilities beyond Thestlen and Valleyner."

"You learned to control the breomer?" Loghleen asked.

"Control is a harsh word," Myrr said. "We learned to inspire them."

"And Sandrovar?" I asked. "Why didn't you show up then?"

"The Nephilins had already butchered the entire city. It was their first act of freedom since they're now allowed to roam these lands." He glanced at Oriah and Loghleen. "No offense."

"I saw him with you, Bellwound." Myrr sat on the ground beside me, my reflection scattered over her armor. "I heard your conversation near the cliff. I heard the promise you made. We can defeat the gods together. Both need you. Your position is one of great power. You rule over the decision of the immortals."

"Rule?" I scoffed. "Does this look like ruling? The Mistrid didn't give me enough strength to protect me from a Shadow bite. I couldn't save Arnon—"

"There are more like you and Kymer," Myrr said with a hint of excitement. "Think about that when you feel defeated."

The pain in my shoulder wasn't enough to hold me down. I was persistent and, once they noticed I meant to stand, Oriah helped me.

"Others?" Kymer muttered. "What others?"

"That's a presumption, Myrr," Quivern said.

"A safe one to make now." Myrr stared at Kymer. "You have a second Mezar. It's safe to assume others were claimed by Lucifer's epistles. We found scrolls in Valleyner, buried deep in the corners of that world."

Kymer clutched the strap of his satchel. His face flushed.

"The gods made us," Quivern added, "but they haven't ruled well over their creation in millennia. That's why we rebelled before this age. When Lucifer was judged before the Regent, we chose defection, seeing how easily we could be betrayed. Our war isn't against crowns, but against minds blindly following them. And now is finally the time to change them."

"Were you Stars once?" Kymer asked. "Like the others?"

"Yes," Myrr said.

"But we bleed the same as you now," Quivern added. "Myrr and I were the first to claim our place after Bellwound's Blood-date."

"Your place?" I asked.

"Here," Myrr said with a smile. "In Thestlen. The divine is still in us, but we chose mortality. We chose to fight in this plane."

Quivern beat a fist over his chest. "We've come to join your quest, god-killer."

"That we have," Myrr agreed. "You have our swords, shields, and wings, Bellwound."

"God-killer," I said. "God-killer…"

"There are those in this world who will listen," Myrr said. "Stay on your course. Go east. Vragner is a good place to gather the Loyal. They may be stubborn at first, but they'll lend you an ear."

"If we do as you say," Oriah said. "Will you join us?"

"We go west," Myrr answered. "The Sindal are crossing the Ghorghon Sea. We'll meet with them first."

"Are we to simply follow your orders?" Loghleen asked. "Go to Vragner blindly, hoping what you say is true?"

"What other proof do you need that we came to fight for the right side?" Quivern sucked a breath between his teeth.

"Apologies if I insulted you," she said. "But the gods and all that have come from them have lied, Fallen or otherwise. While you were locked up in some remote corner in Valleyner, my kind lived underground, taught that the whole reason why we were created was to aid Lucifer when he returned to avenge his fall. There are so many sides and all that lies in between."

"We believed the lessons and teachings Helstrid and Reemon shared," Oriah said. "But then we, too, started thinking for ourselves and went off on our own journey."

"And that's why I must insist you listen," Quivern said. "You lived in this world, but you were not a part of it. We saw kingdoms rise and fall while you were buried beneath the earth."

"And we did so because we listened to Helstrid and Reemon," Loghleen rebutted. "We simply obeyed orders and were deprived of the chance to be a part of this world. That shouldn't be held against us. All I'm saying is, it's hard to trust, even those you've known an entire existence."

Her eyes landed on me. She held Oriah's hand.

"I have one question before we agree to fight together," Oriah said. "And the god-killer can accept our request or decline it."

"What's your request?" I asked.

"That though we come from different minds, we'll remember our true enemies. We've all lived different journeys, believed different tales, and trusted in lies. As truth dawns upon us all, we will stand together willingly."

"And part in free will if needed," Loghleen added.

"What's your answer, Bellwound?" Oriah asked.

"I accept."

"You talk as if you're expecting all of us to fall," Kymer said.

"The gods fell into their own trap," Loghleen said. "We're creation. We may fall into the same fate. I just want to make sure that if the fight strays from our common cause, we will have the freedom to part without strife."

Myrr approached her, laid a fist on her chest, and said, "I understand that once freedom has been tasted, one is willing to fight for it at all costs. I'll abide by your request, Nephilin. May our minds remain free as we join under a common cause."

"To protect mortals," Quivern added.

"And to kill the gods," I said.

Quivern banged a fist on his chest. "For crowns and stars."

"For crowns and stars," we all said together.

ORIAH

CHAPTER EIGHTEEN

It had been three days since Myrr and Quivern's departure. While we waited for Bellwound's recovery, he and Kymer shared life stories, talked about their Mezars, and their lives before their quests.

I didn't mind not being invited to most of their conversations. They had found something in common, like Loghleen and me—a cause that bound them together.

I spent most of my time by the ruins near the river, sitting on a stone bench under the remains of a round gazebo. Vines had been carved into its six columns and its roof mirrored entangled roots, with crevices that gave way for the light of the sun to come through. The columns, pillars, and statues around me were reminders of an ancient world that existed long before. I was alive when this place had experienced its full glory before whatever war destroyed their homes. Only I was underground, hidden, clinging to the truth Helstrid and Reemon passed down to my kind.

The Sindal reminded me of myself when I first started asking questions. It was the whispers of hidden tales that stirred in me the desire to leave Sandrovar behind—claims that there was more to the stories this world had come to know. Loghleen followed me not just because of our love, but because she, too, enjoyed the freedom to choose.

Helstrid and Reemon preached doctrine that had us waiting for the day where Lucifer would return for vengeance, as if waiting was our greatest reward. In the same way Bellwound and Arnon were in the dark about their truth, I had been in darkness about mine.

No doctrine, story, or prophecy talked about our parents. They were turned to Shadow at one point. We knew that much. Even as centuries turned into ages, I still tried to dig deep into my mind, hoping to find any hint of what mine looked like. Was my mother the Star? My father the human? Perhaps it was the other way around. I had found freedom in choice, but the chains of my past kept me bound.

"You wonder what happened here." Loghleen's voice surprised me. "You wonder what these people believed." She approached one of the columns of the gazebo. "I see these ruins." Her fingertips trailed over the carved vines. "The memory of beauty and glory, and I think about the things we missed, the things we lost without knowing they belonged to us."

"I can tell your mind has been far, my love," I said. The rays of the sun brushed her golden locks and eyes. "You've been somewhat quiet and, dare I say, a little distant since the Sindal left."

"Sometimes our thoughts beg us to be alone with them," she

said, eyes following the vine pattern. "My thoughts have been entangled like these vines. Thoughts of fear. The fear of following orders again." Her footsteps rustled the dry leaves scattered on the stone floor of the gazebo. "Like we did with Helstrid."

"The Sindal didn't order us to do anything."

"But we're trusting in strangers. We trusted Helstrid and lived locked away in the darkness. We trusted the Council and look what happened. Perhaps, deep in my mind, I thought this would be a chance for us to trust in ourselves."

"My love." I beckoned her closer with a wave. She sat on my lap. "The Sindal may be strangers, but our common cause makes us allies. We will trust them with our cause, not with all our secrets. They're of Valleynerian descent. We're—"

"Fallen." She kissed my forehead.

"Do you regret leaving our underground kingdom in Sandrovar? Do you ever wonder what would've happened had we stayed? All the things we had been preparing for are happening now."

"I regret trusting those who failed us. I don't regret our promise to the Throvars and Helvugs. But we're nearing a time when all our journeys will be split into different paths."

"*Our* journeys?" I repeated.

"Love may bind us to one another," she said. "But not even love can defeat death in the end, can it? We're immortals, but if metal pierces us, we still die. Our paths fork after death if one of us stays behind."

"Why are you saying this?"

"Do you trust me?" she asked, holding my face between her hands.

"With my life," I replied, confused.

"Do you trust that whatever I've revealed and whatever I've kept hidden from you was for the sake of our love?" Her eyes glistened.

Silence.

"I need you to answer me." Her chin quivered.

"You've followed me out of Sandrovar. You followed me into the Council. Of course, I trust your reasons."

A tear raced down her cheek. "If we're ever to part, I want you to know I'll still be fighting for us. In this world or the next." Our lips met. I knew her kiss. I knew her touch. I knew her heartbeat. Her lips were hesitant, her hands frightened, and her heartbeat too fast.

She pressed her forehead against mine, held my face between her hands, and sang a familiar song.

Night star in the sky, how marvelous you shine.
Above me you stand.
In the darkness, you are the only lamp.
Even if small and dim,
Night star, even in shadow, you bring light from within.

A ferocious roar pierced the air. Loghleen jolted to her feet. Another screech, more high-pitched this time. Two winged shadows crossed the gray skies. Dragons.

"By the feather," I mumbled as the creatures screeched, the wind cast by their wings striking my face. Distant marching joined the roaring while I observed the winged beasts reflected in her expectant eyes. Was she ready for their arrival? No, no. That wasn't possible.

She pulled me by the wrist, racing back to camp. I followed her, my thoughts at war.

Bellwound and Kymer were on edge, watching the winged beasts in the sky.

"Dragons?" Bellwound shouted. "Fucking dragons?"

"*Desert* dragons," Kymer said. "The kind you don't want to fuck with. The beasts are starved and then released during battle."

The trees on the other side of the river swayed. The riverbank didn't remain empty for long. Armored Shadows formed a line, screaming and growling like starved dogs. Bellwound had a hard expression on his face. He was probably trying to peer into their minds, but he seemed frustrated as he surveyed the riverbank.

One desert dragon circled above while the other flew down in our direction. Its hide was the color of sand, glistening as its hind legs sunk beneath the shallow water. The dragon's front legs were strong, their muscles defined. The animal shook its neck, roaring as its black eyes searched the four of us. Helstrid was its rider. She alighted from the creature, attired in a long black cloak. Her breasts, shoulders, and arms were protected by a dark armor. On her chest was the symbol of my people.

A somber silence settled.

"Well, isn't this lovely?" she asked with a chuckle. "To have all of us gathered here on our return from Vragner. You lot are always late, from what I can see. I'm afraid you missed seeing a much bigger army. It would've been quite a sight to behold."

"You bitch," Bellwound said. "You killed them?"

"No, no, no," she said. "Not all of them. We need a few human rulers to aid us. But most of the civilians are now on the other side of this river." She raised a finger as if remembering something. "Did you all enjoy our little parting gift in Sandrovar? I hope the dead didn't bother you too much. Oh, and Bellwound? Reemon is hovering above us right now. Would you like to say hello to Arnon's shell?"

"You *are* a bitch, aren't you?" Kymer stepped forward. "Riding high on your big leather bird, prancing about like you're some expensive mare."

The desert dragon snarled behind her, as if understanding Kymer's insult. Helstrid's cheeks were flushed. The frown on her face sent Kymer to his knees.

"I'd show a little respect..." Her words faded as confusion took over her piercing gaze. Her confidence disappeared as Kymer stood to his feet, chest puffed, rage in his eyes. Her unseen powers had no effect on him.

"Who are you, boy?"

"Maybe your worst nightmare," Kymer said.

She turned her eyes to me, squinting while trying to strike me with her unseen power. It failed. The dragon trudged forward, its roar a shield keeping Helstrid protected while she fled back toward the beast.

I unsheathed my sword as she climbed on its back. I followed, using the dragon's thigh as a platform to jolt me forward. The creature took to the sky, but not before I plunged my blade into its hide. I held on to the pommel of the sword as it let out a pain-filled screech. The beast's tormented sound beckoned the other desert dragon closer.

Helstrid held on to the dragon's spikes, chancing a look over her shoulder. A hint of pain crawled into my body as we flew further from the others, growing stronger with our distance. My grip weakened as the pain intensified. Death would find me if I plunged into the Shadows gathered at the riverbank.

The reflection of the dragon tainted the waters of the river below. The roars of the Shadows loudened as we neared them. I had no time. I let go.

The water was cold, so cold it felt like daggers scraping my bones. The two winged silhouettes in the sky were visible even from beneath. I quickly swam back to the surface. The beasts had found ground with their followers. On one side, a Shadow army; in the air, two desert dragons; and on the other, my love and companions.

When I was a young boy, I always imagined myself being here in this very moment, fighting for the cause I was taught to believe in. The dragons and Shadows had long been the prize. Now they had become enemies of my freedom.

The defiant roars and shouts suddenly grew into screeches and whimpers, like dogs scared of a wild beast. The trees behind

Bellwound, Kymer, and Loghleen swayed violently. The two desert dragons roared from the other side, flapping their wings like fighting roosters, flames erupting from their open jaws.

They took to the skies from the trees, with white wings wreathed in light. Their glass-like armor gave them away. The Sindal had come.

The dragons ascended toward them. The Shadows found courage again, screaming and roaring while I swam back to the others. A few of them were without armor. They plunged into the water, swimming my way.

The two dragons fought the Sindal with fire. I swam faster as the Shadows approached behind me. I was their prey.

One of the desert dragons plummeted toward me, two Sindal on its tail. It swooped over the water, trying to ensnare me with its clawed feet, but a Sindal warrior sunk a blade into its neck before it reached me. Blood spewed on my head: black, warm, and putrid. The creature soared, but its armored rider fell in the river.

The Sindal dove into the water like eagles, ensnaring the swimming Shadows by their neck and arms, tearing them apart like parchment. Soon the river flowed black and the air smelled foul.

I reached the shore. Loghleen hugged me.

"You're alright," she said, lips on mine. "You're alright."

"What the fuck do you want?" Bellwound said behind gritted teeth. I followed his gaze over my shoulder. Reemon marched out of the water, armor dripping, his scarlet eyes piercing behind his horned helmet.

"And here I thought your armor would've forced you to the bottom," I said while Helstrid approached behind him, mounted on her dragon, the beast landing in the shallow water.

"We can't have everything we want, now can we?" he said in a gravelly voice, still sounding somewhat like Arnon. "Had it been so, many things would be different." He smirked, arching his right eyebrow upward.

Bellwound had a determined expression on his face that was a mixture of pain and rage as he fully concentrated on Reemon.

"What?" Reemon shrugged. "You still see Arnon in my face? I'm afraid that won't change. You'll always see him when you look at me."

Bellwound's posture grew stiff as he took in a breath through his teeth, clenching his hands into fists.

"Can you strike the face of the one you claim to love?" Reemon asked.

Bellwound's body slouched forward, his fists slackening at Reemon's question.

"His memories are mine." Reemon's tongue traced over his teeth. "The more I become a part of his body, the more I see them. And the more they fade."

"Stop taunting him," Loghleen said. "Please."

Reemon grunted. "I assume you're ready to come along then? We must be off."

My heart was a stone thrown and forgotten at the bottom of a lake. "What does he mean?"

"Do you still trust me?" Loghleen's voice wavered.

"You're going with him?" It hurt to even say the words.

She looked deep into my eyes. "Do you still trust me?"

"Loghleen." Her name was my only argument.

"I followed you out of Sandrovar. I followed you to the Council. I've always trusted you. I ask that you keep on trusting me, my love."

I held up both her hands and kissed them, fighting my tears away—they were the real answer to her question. I didn't know what it meant not to trust her. I didn't expect my trust to be shattered so suddenly. How could I say aloud the words that would confirm the departure of my love?

Helstrid's dragon roared, spreading out its wings, threatening us as she alighted from the creature.

"Loghleen," she said. "We need to go."

The welling tears made the blue of her eyes shimmer even brighter. She mouthed the words "I love you" and walked toward Helstrid, climbing on the dragon. Reemon followed, sitting behind her.

Watching the beast fly away brought on an emptiness I had never felt before. Since we had made our love known to each other, life had always been planned, built, and dreamed with us together. Even when we believed Helstrid and Reemon's doctrines, we did so together. We had loved together. We rebelled together. And now we'd die apart.

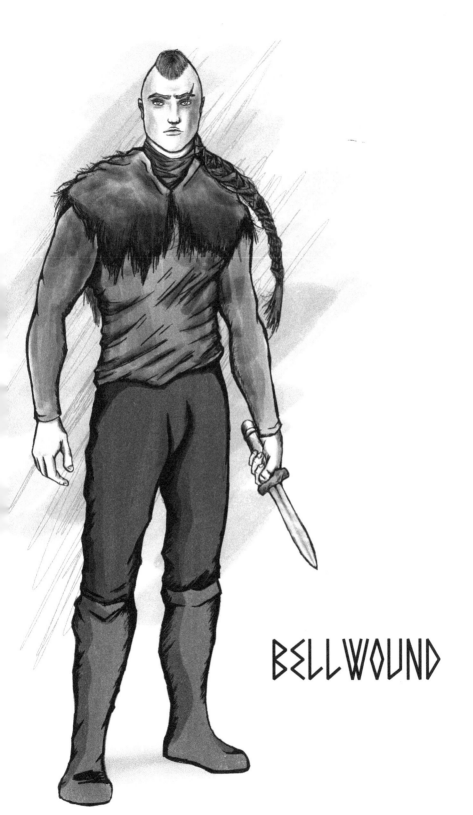

BELLWOUND

CHAPTER NINETEEN

A cloud of ash scattered in the sky as the Sindal continued to destroy the Shadows. The three of us remained quiet, watching the battle with an eerie stillness. It was a beautiful and haunting sight to witness. The light cast by the Sindal's wings created a deathly spectacle. Every woosh of a blade, every roar and groan was muffled noise in my ears. Loghleen had left. The heaviness of Oriah's heart was reflected in his eyes, empty and lost.

We remained by the riverbank, sitting under a few trees until the sun and the silence started to set. I dug deep into my mind, trying to find words of comfort, but I couldn't understand what he felt. My eighteen years were a drop in the bucket of his life. I kept opening my mouth, hoping to say something clever or something that would ease his pain.

"You don't have to say anything," Oriah finally said, sitting to my left. "Let me mourn."

"Loghleen is alive," I said.

"So is Arnon, it seems," he said, deadpan. "Alive somewhere. They may be living, but our paths are no longer the same. Even in life, we may not be with them ever again."

"Are we just going to sit here?" Kymer said from my right. "Moping around? I am tired of watching those hideous things explode into ash."

Oriah didn't move.

"I get that it's tough," Kymer continued. "For all of us. But the longer we stay here, the more people will die." He jumped to his feet. "I know the Sindal suggested Vragnar, but what if we go even farther?" His hands were on his waist, eyeing me like he had solved a mystery. "What if there are answers in the far east? In Winghorn?"

"What answers?" I asked.

"My uncle Trun was a scribe there in his youth, living in the Temple of the Wise. He shared a story once, a few days before he died. A man visited him with a scroll. He never showed his face, but he asked my uncle to copy the scroll, something about there being power in his handwriting. He was masked when he dropped off the parchment and kept his face hidden when he picked it up. He warned that the tale was prophecy. He told me the story and said only two copies had ever been made. One for the faceless wanderer and another for the temple."

"What did it say?"

"It was called 'The Man in Gray.' It was a prophecy, about the rise of the one who would defeat those who tipped the scales of the universe."

"The gods," I mumbled.

"He'd command armies and lead mortals and Valleynerians against both light and darkness." Kymer ran a hand over his mouth. "The story called this being a god-killer."

"God-killer. There's that word again."

"I know. I thought my uncle was just rambling on about random stories. He was drunk when he told the tale. But there may have been some truth to it."

"What else do you remember from the story?" Oriah asked.

"Just this passage," Kymer said. "He shared it only once, but I remember it as if he'd told it to me yesterday. My uncle said it was a passage from a book that is yet to be written." His face grew vacant as he recalled the memory. "'Let us make mankind in our image, in our likeness, so they may rule over the fish in the sea and the birds in the sky, over the livestock and all the wild animals, and over all the creatures that move along the ground.'"

"A new world," I said.

"Trun was your uncle then." Footsteps rustled from the woods.

"Quivern," I said, his face and armor covered in mud and blood.

"And just when I thought you lot had left us," Oriah said, standing to his feet.

"He was an honorable man," Quivern said

"You?" Kymer folded his arms. "You were the hooded man? You saw him at the temple?"

"Like I said before, siding with neither Lucifer nor the Creator gave us time to seek other truths. The universe holds many secrets."

"What else did this prophecy say?" I asked.

A look of disappointment crossed Quivern's face. "I don't know. I couldn't understand the wording on the parchment." His gaze shifted to Kymer. "And if your uncle's words about this prophecy are true, then he most likely found a way to read it while at the Temple of the Wise. It's not easy to decipher the language of the Regent."

"How did you know he was copying prophecy if you didn't understand what it said?" Oriah asked.

"Because we stole it from the vault of the Regent," he replied with pride. "We knew the context, the god-killer, and the quotes from a book in the future. There had to be truth to it since the scroll was well protected."

"Why did you need a copy then? And why a mortal?" Kymer asked.

"A copy so the Regent wouldn't notice its absence. Human hands had to write the words so the scroll could never be tracked." He waved a hand at me and Kymer. "Take the Mezars for example. Fashioned by Lucifer himself. Both can be tracked by Valleynerian forces."

"The gods keep tricking us," I said. "First Hanell with his justified glory and secrecy, then Lucifer having more than one Mezar. They'll never stop, will they?"

"To be fair, we are their creations," Quivern said.

"There are many things a creator has no control over," I said. "A painter may paint a beautiful picture, but it has no power over the flames that destroy it. Perhaps we're the flames this world needs."

"Go to Winghorn," Quivern said. "If there are any survivors in Vragner, my kind will tend to them. Take the road to the south in case any of our enemies are still lingering in this area. Go to the Temple of the Wise. Stay there until I find you."

CHAPTER TWENTY

Trees were exchanged for bare valleys after four days on the road. Except for the sway of the low grass or the ripple of a stream, nothing moved. The mountains on the horizon were rocky, their peaks hidden in the clouds. The days got colder, the nights longer. We had no soft surfaces to rest on, no animals to hunt.

Oriah got a fire going every night by means of a flamewarp, a gray shrub that glistened as if covered in gems. The landscape was overrun with them. He used rocks to spark its tiny leaves together every night until they were set aflame. He slept away from us, beside a fire of his own. I imagined that in his mind, Loghleen was still with him at night. He barely spoke after her departure.

Every night before I fell asleep, I hoped to see Arnon again. I wondered if what I had seen was a dream or vision. Had our kiss been real? Had it all happened in my head?

To interrupt my mental suffering, I'd touch the Mezar. Calm, that's what it brought me. I also hoped to see Lucifer and the Creator again. I needed a revelation—something that proved which stories were true.

Stories. At this point, I loathed them. Stories were twisted for someone else's reward and despised by those challenged by them. Every meaningful story that had given me a foundation turned out to be a lie. I had no other choice but to write my own.

We stumbled upon a pool of hot water on the seventh day. A welcomed surprise. To our relief, a tree of berrycharm grew out of the rocky terrain near the water. It was so heavy with fruit, its branches warped down. We set up camp beneath it since its leaves were wide enough to cast a nice shade. It was also within a reasonable distance from the spring for privacy.

Oriah bathed while Kymer and I sat beneath the shade, indulging on berries.

"Ever been in love?" Kymer asked with a handful of fruit.

"So out of nowhere," I said, popping a berry into my mouth.

"What was? The question or love?"

"Both."

He scooched closer. "So?"

"Yes." My gazed turned to the twisted roots of the berrycharm tree sticking out of the rocks. "I still am, actually."

He tossed a berry in his mouth.

"Arnon... Arnon was my best friend before being host to a Fallen Star." I sighed. "If only love withered when people were distant. Oriah wouldn't be suffering. I wouldn't be wondering if Arnon still lived in the Dark Beyond like Hanell and Lucifer claim."

"Still a virgin?" he asked.

"With all that's happening around us, that's what you want to know?"

A shy smile took his lips. He shuffled in place, rubbed his neck, and said, "I'm trying to pretend like everything is alright. Like maybe we did go to that pub in Erchmon and talked about life as if no darkness had come for us."

His eyes begged me to go along with the charade. I obliged. I didn't mind pretending with him for a bit. I welcomed the escape.

"Not a virgin." I smirked.

He shot another berry into his mouth.

"What about you?" I asked. "Ever been in love?"

"Yes." He slouched forward, elbows on his knees. "With my dragon back home."

We shared a laugh, but I couldn't help but notice his hand grabbing his crotch. At first, I thought it was just him unsticking his balls, but he did it three more times.

"I've never loved anyone," he said. "But you don't need love for a good time, now do you? I have plenty of those tales."

"Experienced then?"

"Very much so."

I leaned back on the rock, folding my hands over my crotch to hide my sudden bulge. His gaze darted between my eyes and my pants.

Oriah returned from the spring, hair dripping. The sight of him lowered the tent between my legs and freed my hands. He sat beside me.

"My turn." I slapped my thighs and jumped to my feet.

I followed the rising steam. The Mezar came along with me. The hot pool of water sprung up through the hole between the black rocks. I removed the satchel from my shoulder, took off my clothes, tossed everything on the edge, and carefully stepped in. It suddenly felt like I was in my tub in Heedeon, watching the autumn leaves drift from their branches.

I slowly untangled my braid—the braid Arnon had done in Heelyan. The act felt like an official departure from my old life. My hands grazed over the sides of my head, the stubs of growing hair prickling at them. There was an eternity between my Blood-date and today. One could hate gods. One could want to kill them. But the pain of a lost life was stronger than any other desire. That's what all the hidden stories and secrets had cost me: my life. Anger subsided as my body relaxed in the heat, my sorrow sinking deeper.

A few of the rocks by the edge were smooth. I swam toward one and reclined against it as dawn crawled across the sky. I liked Kymer's idea of pretending, so I shut my eyes. I was back in Heelyan, dancing with Arnon, masks on our faces, our bodies rubbing together. I recalled the feeling of his bulge against mine. Memory then took me back home, to the summer days when we'd go swimming. The trail of hair on his stomach that led into his pants. I had always wanted to follow that path.

I grabbed myself, keeping my eyes shut so the memories wouldn't be disturbed. No god was in my mind. No nightmare. I wanted to pretend he was there.

A splash in the water brought me back to reality. Kymer was across from me, naked. His shoulders were broad, chest defined. He had a round birthmark right above his bellybutton. His legs—and what was between them—was hidden under the water.

"Are we busy?" he asked with a smirk.

I had no urge to hide what I was doing. My grip remained tight as he looked at me, his hand crawling across his stomach. He, too, had a trail of hair, thicker than Arnon's. His hand followed it, casting soft ripples as it moved back and forth.

"And what's keeping you so busy?" he asked with a shudder.

I could tell him the truth. I could tell him I was thinking about Arnon. That I was pretending he was there. But maybe I could use him in my pretending.

"You know where my hand is," I said. "You're smart enough to figure it out."

He swam closer, gaze locked onto my own. The closer he got, the more tension I felt.

There was still enough light in the sky for me to catch a glimpse of him under the water. He was hard and ready, his foreskin pulled back, revealing his purple head.

"Turn around," he said, touching my right shoulder.

I stood and did as he requested. I stiffened and throbbed more as his cock grazed the cheeks of my arse, stiff and long. His breath brushed the nape of my neck as he curled his fingers in my hair.

"Arnon," I whispered behind a shudder.

He braided my hair. I didn't dare move. His touch felt good.

Soothing. His lips found my neck once he finished the single braid. My fingers stroked his thigh under the water, moving to his arse, begging him to press against me even harder.

His finger forced my face toward his, my body followed. Our lips were a thread away from each other. The heat of his skin bounced off my own.

"Can I kiss you?" His voice trembled with longing.

I wasn't gentle. My lips found his fast. His hands were on my waist, pressing our bodies together, grinding. I explored both of his arse cheeks, finding my way between them. He gently bit my bottom lip, setting my entire body on fire.

I took one of his nipples in my mouth. He moaned. I licked my fingers to play with the other. My heart raced. One of my hands followed the trail of hair down his stomach, finding the throbbing prize. I stroked it, earning grunts and moans of pleasure.

He gently urged me to sit on the edge of the smooth rock, my other head now level with his face. He smirked before his lips met my stomach. He kissed his way down until his lips were wrapped around me. I had almost forgotten what it felt like to be immersed in warmth. My base repeatedly met the chill air, contrasting the light suction and safe dance of his tongue.

He was gentle at first but grew more determined once my hand was in his hair, guiding his movements and speed. His tongue knew its way around, moving in circles, following the fold of my foreskin. With a gentle tap, I beckoned him to look up.

"Your turn." I jumped back into the water.

He took my place on the rock. My face went between his legs. The hair at the end of his trail brushed the tip of my nose as he begged me to keep everything inside. I did as he requested, choking, but compliant.

He finished first, purging pleasure into my mouth. He wanted the same from me, and I obliged. Night had already taken the sky, but we remained in the pool, arms wrapped around each other, counting stars until we decided to return to camp.

It was good to pretend.

CHAPTER TWENTY-ONE

Oriah woke us up before dawn and insisted we be on our way so we could arrive at the village of Aleeon before nightfall. The possibility of sleeping on an actual bed was enough to get me on my feet.

Kymer had slept beside me the entire night. We hadn't touch each other after we got back to camp. Not to say I wasn't tempted to do what we did one more time, both the sex and the pretending.

The three of us plucked a few berries from the berrycharm tree and were on our way. Kymer didn't talk much. He'd look at me and smile, but not for too long, taking care to ensure his thoughts didn't reflect in his eyes.

My mind wavered between him and Arnon as we carried on. The rocky terrain gave way to trees and shrubs, but my thoughts remained the same. Arnon had spent a life by my side, and yet I had never experienced with him what I did with Kymer. I felt like a fool for thinking about such things. The doom of the world was on hand after all.

Not much was shared between the three of us. Our minds were off to places of their own until we finally came upon a hill overlooking a village in a valley at sundown. It had no walls and, at first glance, I thought a painting had come to life right before my eyes. Though small, I could tell those that had settled there tried not to pillage the greenery, but to respect it. Roots and branches and rocks sprang from the muddy streets and quaint wooden houses.

Oriah tore a piece of fabric from the hem of his shirt. "Here." He handed the torn cloth to me. "Wrap it over my eyes."

"Your eyes?" I asked.

"The village is small. We need a place to eat and sleep. We don't need my eyes drawing attention and stirring up questions."

"What's our story?" Kymer asked as I tied a knot behind Oriah's head. He looked at me fleetingly, struggling to keep his attention away.

"If someone asks," I said. "We're leading our blind friend home. They shouldn't ask much after that."

"Can you see through the cloth?" Kymer asked.

"Yes," Oriah replied. "But guide me down the hill. There may be guards. We don't want them sniffing out our act."

Kymer held Oriah's hand as we took the muddy trail down the hill toward the homes and market. People chattered and bought goods and drank, not really minding our presence. Long-necked hens crossed the street and a few purple-beaked ducks insisted on swimming in the small shallow ponds on the ground.

Two armored guards watched the street, bearing the sigil of a sword cutting through a book on their chests. But no armor was enough to keep my attention away from the herd of horned rabbits that leapt out of the shrubs to cross the street. There were five of them, led by one plumper and bigger than the rest.

Four of them carried on, but their leader halted, standing on its hind legs. Its dark round eyes looked at me, nose wriggling. Had I been home, the rabbit would've been food. But out here, the animal was a welcomed visitor from my past.

The horned rabbit squealed, gasped for breath, and fell on its side as a dagger pierced its stomach. "Dinner is served," said the approaching guard with a smirk, his companion beside him. "You see, they're not from here. Merchants from this small Metranian village bring these up here. They eat our crops. Pests, if you ask me."

"I've had them before," I said. "They're delicious."

"Indeed, they are," said the companion. "Blessed be the Lion." His hand wrapped around the hilt of the sword at his waist. Bear pelts were on his shoulder. A long, dirty red cape draped down his back.

"Blessed be," Oriah said.

"I've never seen you lot here before," he continued. "You just arrived?"

"We're passing through," Kymer said. "We're taking our friend home to Winghorn. Thieves robbed him and took his eyes."

The companion scrunched his face. "Sorry to hear that. Where'd you all come from?"

"West," Oriah said.

"Where in the west?" the guard insisted, his words suddenly heavy with impatience. "Vragner?"

"Yes," I replied quickly—too quickly. I had opened a floodgate for questions had word of Vragner's destruction reached his ears. "We've been walking for days. We've slept on bare soil. We haven't had a decent meal aside from desert fruit. We're hoping to find some food and shelter for the night. We'll be off in the morning." Maybe he'd pity us now.

"If you would follow me," he ordered, waving farewell to his companion.

He led us through the village as the sun set, to the edge of the forest. The foliage was denser. The tall trees and small thorny shrubs made it hard to navigate. Puddles of mud and fallen pine trees were scattered along the rugged terrain. The guard was patient as we guided Oriah. Or perhaps he was observant, hoping to spot any action that triggered more questions. Sometimes Oriah would deviate from something before we warned him or pulled him in the right direction. I feared his actions made the guard see right through us.

Amidst this gloomy landscape was an old shack. We followed the guard inside. The fireplace was lit, and the smell of newly brewed barley tea reached my nostrils.

A girl was inside, sitting on a lonely chair by the fire. She jumped to her feet, startled. Her clothes were tattered and dirty. Her eyes were each a different color—one gray and one green. She wore a scarf around her neck, and to cover her hands, she had on a ragged pair of gray fingerless gloves. A two-strap leather bag was at the foot of her chair.

"My name is Abhel," said the guard. "And this here is Serrida. She showed up this afternoon, heading to your destination. Winghorn. Coincidence, maybe?"

"I know you doubt me," Serrida said. "But I spoke the truth."

"You know them?" Abhel asked.

"We've never—"

Abhel raised a hand, halting Kymer's words. "I asked the girl."

"I've never seen them," Serrida said haltingly. "I don't know them. I told you the truth. I have family in Winghorn."

"So does the blind blond." The guard pointed at Oriah. "Interesting how easy it was for him to walk through that thick patch of vegetation. And to add to this coincidence, you have all come from Vragner." The guard circled us like a predator. "From what I hear, it wasn't men or women who killed that entire city in a day."

I struggled to keep my composure.

"Winghornians and Vragnerians have been fighting for the land between us for years," he said. Serrida slowly picked up the bag by the foot of her chair, laying it on her lap. "Twenty Winghornian soldiers—*my* men—went to Vragner about three weeks ago. We got a note from a watchbird today informing of the city's destruction. I was told to keep an eye out for strange folk heading this way. And here you are."

"You have every reason to be suspicious of wanderers," Oriah said. "I'll give you the truth then. The monsters are real. The Fallen are here."

"I had no doubt about that," Abhel replied calmly. "I never doubted the return of the Dove. I just never thought I'd be alive to see it."

Oriah removed the cloth from his eyes. Abhel was shocked. He gazed at Oriah's eyes as if they were gems.

"These are dire times. Ever thought you'd lay eyes on a Nephilin?" Oriah asked.

He studied Oriah's features closely then walked to a wooden table placed under an iron-cast chandelier. He sat on the chair at the far end and invited us to do the same with a wave. "I'm sure you don't mind a brief chat. My men never returned. The ones that did were dead. Their bodies washed ashore this morning. Our kids found them while playing by the river."

Out the window behind Abhel, a gentle breeze set the branches of the trees to dancing, but a few rattled to a different rhythm. My breathing faltered. Golden eyes pierced the dark vegetation. A little boy frantically crawled up a tree, eyes set on the shack. My body tensed as its scraggly lips pulled into a smile. We had been found already, but by no mere child. Gone too soon, he had become one of them. The Shadows were here.

My first instinct was to enter his mind, but I was defeated. Doubt gripped me suddenly. Had I been able to do it, I would've killed the little boy. He couldn't be more than nine. He didn't deserve to die—neither as a Shadow nor as a human. What was the use of divinity without heart? Or was it my heart that kept me from using it at all?

The walls of the shack trembled. Claws pierced the roof, ripping it open. Flapping wings the color of sand blew us off our feet and onto the ground. A desert dragon. Abhel was its prey. It ensnared him between its jaws, breaking him apart with two bites. An armored Shadow was mounted on the beast. It hissed as the dragon feasted on flesh.

The four of us darted out of the shack. I chanced a look back. Another desert dragon appeared in the orange sky, chasing us as we ran through the vegetation. We had the cover of trees, but the dragon had fire. It spewed out flames, torching the trees.

Oriah grabbed Serrida's arm and tossed her on his back. I did the same with Kymer. We had no time for mere human speed. Oriah and I ran beside each other, dodging fire, trees, and rocks as screams echoed from the village.

A body plunged from the air to the ground, falling ahead of me and disappearing between shrubs still unscathed by the flames. I ran past it, recognizing the face of the man. Da.

I halted so fast, Kymer launched off my back. I grabbed his wrist in mid-air and dropped him on the ground before he flew into the fire. Oriah stopped beside me.

"Why are we stopping?" Serrida asked, arms around Oriah's neck.

"We can't linger," Oriah said. "We have to keep on going."

"That's my father," I said. "That's him…"

"Bellwound." Kymer grabbed my wrist. "We're going to die if we stay here."

I jerked myself free from his grip and rushed to the body, disregarding the inferno around me. He was wrapped in black rags stained with blood. His eyes were wide, his face blue and swollen. Some of his teeth were missing. Two fingers had been cut off from his right hand.

"Da… What…" My hand went for the Mezar inside my satchel, longing for comfort. "What…"

From the corner of my eye, I spotted the little boy I had seen at the shack standing a few feet away. The flames engulfed the trees behind him, but he was unbothered. Dancing shadows were cast over his face, the fire revealing a gash across his head.

Then I felt it. The pull. The draw. My mind was inside his own. But there was nothing. Just a void I couldn't pierce. Was he really a Shadow then?

A loud hiss brought me back. Da's eyes were no longer black. They were gold. His body writhed on the ground, the veins in his neck bulging. The little boy slowly lifted his hand, fingers spread wide. The higher his hand got, the more Da suffered. He was turning into one of them.

I glanced back. A wall of fire was now between me and my way back to the others. In the blink of an eye, the little boy stood before me. The sound of voices crept into my ears. They begged for mercy.

Everything went dark with the pressure on my face. Was the boy gripping it? Was Da holding it?

Silence was my only answer.

CHAPTER TWENTY-TWO

Thick metal chains surrounded my wrists and ankles. The gray sky rumbled with thunder. A piercing draft of cold air hung about as my senses returned.

My thigh. The pain was excruciating. A blade with ragged edges, transparent like ice, glinted as my sight cleared. A scarlet streak spread down my leg, creating a puddle on the white marble floor. The weapon was almost fully lodged into my flesh.

I was on a balcony, surrounded by thick cloisters. A mist hovered over the city below. The shingled roofs of the houses were just visible among the white, stretching into the horizon.

I tried jerking my right wrist free, but I had no strength. There were bruises all over my body. Every piece of clothing but my black pants had been ripped off.

"Oriah! Kymer! Serrida!" My breath came out as rising steam. I was discouraged, but not ready to believe the worse had happened.

Then a headache surged—a kind I had never felt before. Was a hand reaching into my skull and pulling my brain out?

"I guess not even the Mistrid blessing is a match for Lucifer's Sacredice blade," said a familiar voice. "How do you like the pain, little Bellwound?" She appeared from my right, walking through the shadows the cloisters cast over the long hallway.

"You bitch," I said in a hoarse voice. "What did you do to the others?"

"Oh, I did nothing," Helstrid quipped, releasing me from her painful grip. I gasped for air as she neared me. "Elistran did all the work. The boy you saw is our Shadow captain. He was joined by the wrexing when he found you in the burning forest. You see, wrexing are invisible to the eye. Not even the Sindal can sense their presence. They finally found their way out of the Dark Beyond, thank the Dove." Pain struck me yet again. "And once they ensnare your senses, they make you lose all sight, sound, and touch."

I grunted, holding back my desire to scream. I wouldn't give her the satisfaction.

"The pain can stop," she said. "The killings can stop." She released me. "It's up to you."

"Where are they?" My lips mumbled the words behind my heavy breathing. "The others?"

"Safe," she said. "For now."

"Do you think you're safe?" My eyes pierced hers.

"Tell me, how did you find the new epistle-keeper? Did he tell you how he found his Mezar?"

We both protested with silence for a moment.

"See?" I said. "Lucifer kept secrets even from you. I thought you were a faithful servant. I thought you would know. Who's to say he is—"

She slapped my face. "Don't you dare talk about our Dove that way! The only reason why the Sacredice blade isn't in your chest is because he forbade it. If he chose to conceal the other Mezars, then I trust he knew better than all of us."

"Where is he then?" Our eyes locked. "Where the fuck is Lucifer? You're out here, doing his bidding. And what about him?"

"Consorting with Reemon." She smirked, probably seeing Arnon's ghost in my eyes. "I can still see your lover boy every time I fuck him." I gasped for air as the pain heightened. "He's mine now. All mine. If only you knew what I do with him in the night. Things that perhaps you always dreamt of doing."

"Does it bother you that you can't kill me?" I said behind gritted teeth.

"I can make you suffer still," she whispered in my ear, bringing on the pain. "Like Arnon's parents. Who do you think tortured them until they offered their little baby to the darkness?"

Anger quickly overcame the pain she inflicted on me.

"We do everything we can to keep the ones we love close," she said.

"Mark my words." My chin trembled. "I will kill you."

"Of course you will." She pecked me on the lips.

She released me from the pain. The echo of her heels striking the floor as she walked away angered me. I searched my surroundings for a way out of my restraints, but there was nothing to aid me.

It didn't take long for Helstrid to return, but she wasn't alone. He was with her: Reemon. My heart rushed as my eyes met his scarlet ones. Much about his facial features still reflected Arnon, but the red eyes always disrupted my delusion. They announced again and again that Arnon was gone from that body.

He unchained my wrists without uttering a single word. He still smelled like him, moved like him. Stubs of hair grew on the sides of his shaved head. The braid was different though, laced in thick sections with thinner braids entwined between them.

Helstrid watched everything as if it were a street performance. He tossed one of my arms over his shoulder and dragged me down the hall, through a doorway, and into a room encircled by tall stained-glass windows depicting landscapes and sunsets. Ancient writing covered the walls, the markings reaching up to the ceiling that served as a canvas for paintings displaying human torture. At the center of the room was a golden throne. A man sat upon it, his left arm reposed on the armrest with his head resting on his hand. Reemon forced me to my knees with a kick and walked to stand in the corner. The pain in my thigh was excruciating.

The man stared as if I were a rare animal inside a cage. He had come to me as a shadow, but now he stood before me in full glory, like the man I had seen in those visions.

Lucifer.

"I didn't want things to be like this," he said in a voice that sounded like a sultry song. "I never wanted any of this to happen."

"All the gods lie for their own benefit. You and Hanell are no different."

"You're angry," he said. "I understand." He looked at Reemon and back at me. "But unlike Hanell, I will tell you the truth like I promised."

"And that explains the dagger in my thigh?" I grunted. "Because you keep your word?"

He stood to his feet. His robes were black, covered in thin circular patterns and stars sewn with golden thread. He walked down the two steps in front of his throne. Flashes of light emerged from behind him, taking the shape of wings—six of them.

"I'm not surprised by how stubborn you are." He placed a hand beneath my chin. A ring was on his thumb, two golden wings connected by a red stone. "You take after your father. You fight for what you believe even when all the odds are stacked against you."

"Don't talk about Da," I said. "Don't you talk about my family, you shit."

"I'm not sorry for the things that happened to you. It was the only way to get you here. It was the only way for me to *be* here." He knelt in front of me and slid the blade out of my thigh.

I let out a long breath. Instant relief.

"Do you know who your family is?" Lucifer's brown eyes pierced mine.

"What a foolish question," I said, standing up with trembling legs.

"Why do you think your parents left Heedeon? Why do you think they chose exile? Why was the Mezar buried under your home?" The rays of light shaped like wings throbbed at his words.

"Why does the Mezar allow you to see things? Why does it grow on you?"

"I wouldn't be standing here if I knew."

"That's why secrets had to be kept from you." He touched my shoulder. "Your mother kept a few of them from the man that raised you as his own." A burning sensation spread up my left arm, like a blunt blade carving flesh. The same skin story on his face appeared on my skin—a rose and a dove. "But it's time you knew."

I took a step back, eyeing the markings.

"What are you doing?" I asked.

"Revealing your birthmark."

I took a second step as the impossible struck me. "Birthmark?"

"We have the same," he said.

Acknowledging the sudden lingering thought felt like a crime. Not only because the family I had known my entire life wasn't real, but because a part of him had lived in me for eighteen years.

"You're my father," I whispered, afraid to believe the words.

"Yes," he said. "I am. The blood of the Dove runs in your veins."

"How..." My hands clenched into fists as my strength slowly returned. I despised myself. "How is that possible? You were locked away for thousands of years."

"Time and blood can be bent and molded, little Bellwound."

"Don't be like your toxic lover and speak in riddles," I said, mind reeling. "If this is why the Mezar was buried under my home and calls to me, then what of the other Mezars?"

"The others are important, but only one epistle carries my heart.

And that one is with you. That one responds to you. I knew you would bring my heart back to me. It was my heart, inside the Mezar you carry, that allowed you to see a certain someone in the Dark Beyond."

"Arnon?"

"You were in no dream, little Bellwound," Lucifer said. "You were in the swamp with him. I promised him he'd be able to see you. I kept my promise to him and allowed you into the swamp, and you brought yourself back. You never belonged with mortals, my son. You belonged with the gods from the beginning. Help me return to my place and join me in yours. The others must rue what they did to me. Open your Mezar. Set my heart free. Help me collect the others."

Sorrow gripped me like a vine covered in thorns. I surveyed my body, aware that every part of me was made of him. A tear ran down my cheek as I took in a long breath, my gaze finding Reemon. Seeing the remaining bits and pieces of Arnon hurt more than Helstrid's torture. But it was his scarlet eyes that revealed the truth to me. There were other paths to take besides the one I was on, other worlds I could perhaps tread. Though Lucifer's revelation reminded me of my family's betrayal, it also proved that none of the paths presented to me would do.

"Father," I said. "May I call you that?"

Lucifer smiled. "Of course, Son."

My heart pounded as I walked closer to him. I had made a decision. I feared it. I loathed it. I needed it.

"Thank you," I said. "Thank you for not hiding the truth from me."

He laid a hand on my shoulder, the other still holding the Sacredice blade.

"We shall stand together, my little dove."

My eyes bore into his. I once read in a book that your entire life flashes before your eyes when you're about to die. You dig so deep that you remember things you thought weren't there anymore. As I gazed at Lucifer's face, a memory I once thought so ordinary invaded my mind. I sat at our table back home, Ma and Da beside me. She had made a roast. Da drank his ale and the fire crackled in the fireplace. Arnon showed up unannounced, bringing with him a cherry cake. Had I remembered this at any other time, I wouldn't have thought the memory was anything special. But right now, as I counted my every breath, it felt as if it was all I had.

I grabbed Lucifer's wrist and forced the Sacredice deep into my chest. My breath escaped me. I expected pain, but I felt numb. My legs were gone. His face blurred and sharpened. Time moved slowly as I fell to the ground.

My heart pounded in my ears. I counted every beat, wondering which one would be my last. My vision gave out, but the thudding continued until silence replaced my every thought.

THE DARK BEYOND
BELLWOUND

A starry sky was above me. The moon was so bright, I could see its craters and shadows. My fingers curled into the damp ground.

"You're here," said a familiar voice.

My heart rushed. My breathing faltered.

He was here with me.

OTHER TITLES BY J.D. NETTO

The Broken Miracle Duology

The Broken Miracle: Part One

The Broken Miracle: Part Two

Henderbell

Henderbell: The Shadow of Saint Nicholas

Henderbell: The Shadow of Saint Nicholas (Special Christmas Edition)

Henderbell: Whispers in the Dark

Anthologies

Saved by the Page: Forty-Five Stories Written

by Readers Saved by Books (Edited by J.D. Netto)

CPSIA information can be obtained
at www.ICGtesting.com
Printed in the USA
BVHW041929260622
640687BV00005B/140